Treachery on Tap

by

Constance Barker

Sign up for Constance Barker's New Releases Newsletter

Chapter One

The Grumpy Chicken is not a typical name for an Irish pub, and a small town about forty-five minutes west of Savannah, GA is not where you would expect to find it. But it is my business and home. Recently, events around here were far from our boring, rural life. You see, our little town of Potter's Mill was turned upside down by the first murder in recent, and not so recent, memory. But with some help from me and a few of my friends, the police found and captured the likely suspects. So last night, as the manager and next in line to inherit the pub, I stayed open late and we all drank a little too much. Which also meant we celebrated well past our usual bed times.

In the middle of the festivities, my computer savvy friend, Ida, hooked a special little camera to her laptop to record video of our pickled egg jar. Yes an inanimate object warranted high tech observation during the night. Eight previous jars have fallen to the floor and shattered for some unknown reason. But that has not prevented anyone from embracing their own theories. Things get weirder when you realize the most popular explanation is that a chicken's ghost is knocking this particular jar over. Personally, I think it is one of the cats that like to visit the pub in search of mice in the back alley. So, to solve the mini mystery of why my expensive glass containers jump to their deaths in the middle of the night, a web camera was employed to record the jar and see what causes it to fall. If and when it does again.

Adding to the late night celebrations, my father Tom, the current pub owner, returned home. He was in Atlanta getting some medical attention for a relentless cough. His health has been poor for a while and he probably should lose some weight. As a result, he has not run the pub in years and that's my job now. But the recent care must have been good since Dad was in the pub early this morning, eager to work and prepare for some surprise visitors later today. That is all he would tell me last night and he was still tight lipped about it this morning. He saw me and said, "Ginger, I was worried you weren't coming down from the apartment. You look tired. Did you get some coffee? And your pretty red hair is a mess."

I moaned. "Two cups. I shouldn't have stayed up so late. Especially with surprise visitors coming."

"Lightweight! When I was your age, and a few pounds lighter, I didn't need sleep." Dad patted his belly as he talked, then pointed to the webcam. "Hey, what's this little robot looking thingy that is staring at our pickled egg jar?"

"Dad, you know the pickled egg jars mysteriously break during the night. Ida set up a camera to record video of the jar, to see what is knocking them over."

"Ginger, you always ignore the obvious. It's our testy chicken ghost. You always try to explain it away. But I've worked in this tavern since I was a spry lil laddie, for almost fifty years, and the chicken spirit does these things. Trust me."

I closed my eyes not wanting to have this discussion with Dad. "I know, but there may be another explanation. I don't want to exaggerate something and scare away any of our regular customers. Not everyone likes the chicken ghost like you do."

There was a knock at the front door. I opened the locked entry to find the town hacker and journalist, two of my friends who helped solved the recent crime. Ida beamed and gushed, "Well, did the jar take a dive?"

I spun to look at it on the counter. "Nope, not this time."

Ida frowned. "Shoot, I was so hoping it happened and that my camera caught it. I already have a special account setup on Youtube to upload videos when we get something."

I said, "I guess someone is convinced that something other than a pesky cat is knocking things over. Otherwise, who would want to watch on Youtube? And I have never seen you in here this early in the morning."

Piper, my journalist friend added, "First, cats are very popular on Youtube. And second, we both wanted to see if the jar committed hara-kiri. But as a journalist, I also remember from last night that your father said you were having some surprise visitors today. It was very cryptic, to say the least. So we didn't want to miss the show. Tom is not known for his people skills, so we are thinking this could be one heck of a floor show coming to town."

I laughed. "I had the same thought when he told me."

"So you still don't know who's coming?" Ida asked.

"Nope. Dad just told me it's a surprise and I'll have to wait for them to get here. In the mean time, you two care to help us clean up and get ready to open? The place was packed last night, I could use a hand."

"Sure, but let me quickly check my video recording first, see if I caught anything even though the jar didn't fall." Ida pointed at the laptop hooked to the camera as she spoke. The she went over and checked her recording, but as expected found nothing.

After that, Piper and Ida were wonderful and

pitched in, even after Dixie, my bartender, showed up for work. Bones, my cook, was true to form and showed up a half hour late. He was unshaven and his clothes were wrinkled. I scolded, "What in the world happened to you? You look like you spent the night in the gutter."

Bones sighed. "I kind of did. Well, in my car. My girlfriend threw me out, *again*. She ran into Abbey last night and, well, she found out that I asked Abbey on a date when I went over to town hall. Bad move and I paid for it."

I raised my eyebrows. "Bad move? I think dumb move is more like it. You okay to work?"

"Yeah. I actually want to work today. Get my mind off my love life."

I laughed. "To be nineteen again! You keep pulling moves like that and you'll have no love life. This is a small town and all the local girls are going to know about this little indiscretion of yours."

Bones looked at me and realized the truth in what I said. I knew because he hung his head and continued, "Well, I guess I can just work more hours then. And I'll save some money if I can't get anymore dates."

Piper was within earshot and I heard her laugh at the conversation. She raised her voice so I could hear her. "Eleven-thirty, you ready to open the doors?"

I yelled back, "Sure, but we need to put the training wheels on Bones. He looks pretty rough around the edges this morning."

Piper responded, "I heard. Bones, I hope you learned your lesson. Well, if not, you will. Both of those girls are never going to let you forget this."

Tom went over to Bones and didn't say a word. He just smacked Bones on the back of the head then walked away.

I went to the front doors and unlocked them, ready for another long day. To make sure the front walk was clean after the street fair yesterday, I poked my head out the entryway and that is when I saw it. An eighteen wheeler truck, parking on Main Street right in front of The Grumpy Chicken. On the side of the trailer was emblazoned The Ghost Hounds. I stepped out onto the sidewalk and gawked as it finished claiming its spot next to the curb.

Dixie must have seen something was up because she eventually followed me outside and joined me on the sidewalk. She blurted out, "Holy sh... Show Hosts! That's that TV show!"

A sport utility vehicle parked behind the big rig and the doors flew open. Dixie's body began to shiver and she screamed. "Zach Black! It's really him!"

I was a little confused, but found the puddle of emotion that used to be my bartender kind of funny. She turned into a teenage girl catching sight of

Justin Bieber. I had to admit, the youngest of the group appeared to be in his late twenties, maybe thirty, and he was the tall, handsome type. The kind most girls swoon over. I looked over at my shaking friend. "Dixie, I'm not sure who these people are, but I can tell you they're not Justin Bieber. So you can stop acting like a fool now."

"Ginger, he's one of the hottest shows on TV. I mean *they're* one of the hottest... well you know."

I eyed her trying not to laugh. The three men approached and stood in front of us. The young handsome one spoke first. "Well, good morning pretty ladies. I'm Zach Black, host of The Ghost Hounds. And these are my two co-hosts: Tyler Fells and Cecil Page. But you probably knew that."

I looked him straight in the eye and replied. "No, not really."

Dixie quivered and had a slightly different response. She spoke so fast I almost didn't understand when she said, "I love your show and I'm your biggest fan. I loved the episode where you found that weird sound coming from that really old furnace."

I turned to look at her and tilted my head towards the front door. Dixie understood and added, "Really nice to meet you! I need to go back to work. I hope to see around."

Zach replied, "Will be hard not to. We're filming inside The Grumpy Chicken."

On hearing this news, Dixie did a weird sort of slow motion jogging mixed with jumping up and down as she made her way back into the tavern, all while squealing, "Oh my gosh!"

I guessed by now these were the surprise guests promised by my father. I addressed Zach. "So you know my father, Tom O'Mallory?"

"Our producers do. They made the arrangements and told us the backstory for your place. It's a perfect spot for us to shoot and we're going to have some fun." Zach scanned the outside of The Grumpy Chicken as he talked. His eyes stopped on our old placard, which proclaims the pub name in hand carved, relief gold letters. It is large and mounted to the building over the front door. While it may have been painted a few times over the years, it is the original signboard from one hundred and fifty years ago.

"Well, come on in then. My father is expecting ya. Welcome to The Grumpy Chicken." I swung my hand towards the front door.

We went inside and to my surprise, Ida and Piper had the same reaction as Dixie. Bones even lit up when he saw them. I guess I was no longer one of the cool kids who are up on all the current television shows. Dad greeted them. "Well, glad you made it. Your going to love our chicken ghost. Come on, I'll show you around." So we showed the trio of hosts our pub but it didn't take long as the place isn't that big.

The oldest of the three TV hosts was Tyler, looking to be in his mid-forties and sporting a full, black beard and a partially bald head. He saw the web camera watching the pickled egg jar and asked. "What's that all about? It's a little strange. You must really like pickled eggs to live stream them."

I began, "That's a long story. We have ..."

But Ida cut me off. "That's not a live stream. I'm recording the jar, to see what's knocking it over at night."

Tyler asked, "That's a lot of work over a jar of pickled eggs. This something that happens a lot in Potter's Mill?"

Ida nodded. "Well in this pub, yes. Eight times in the last couple of months. The most popular theory is our ghost chicken is knocking it over. You know, in retaliation for pickling the chicken eggs. So we're recording to see if we can find anything during the night. It always happens late at night."

Tyler eyed the area. "This might be a good spot to wire with EMF and sound meters." I frowned at Tyler's comment, concerned. He noticed me and responded. "Electromagnetic fields. We often detect them when spirits appear. It's safe, just some meters to look for magnetic fields and sounds."

"Oh, that sounds a little safer then." I tried to hide my anxiety. I had a bar to run and it was starting to sound like this surprise was going to be a real pain. "How long do you take to shoot an episode?"

Zach laughed. "You looking to get rid of us already? Don't worry, we usually shoot late at night and should stay out of your hair. The spirits like to appear when everyone is sleeping."

"I do have a business to run, so yeah, I'm a little worried."

Piper spoke up. "Ginger, this show is going to make everyone who lives in Georgia want to be at The Grumpy Chicken. You'll probably need a bouncer to work the front door. This is going to be good for business."

Zach took the opportunity to turn to Tyler. "What are you doing, man? The egg jar is not that interesting and you always try to find an excuse to use your toys. *I* pick the locations and stories to shoot. You know that."

Tyler's face became taught. "No you don't. We're co-hosts, remember. And the jar story is better than just about anything you've ever done."

Zach moved to stand just in front of Tyler, standing close so their noses almost touched. "I pick the shoot locations. End of conversation."

Fortunately, while we talked and escorted the hosts around the tavern, the television crew began to unload. One of them came over to the quarreling co-hosts. He was an older man, in his mid-fifties, and in good shape as evident by his Popeye sized arms. He pried himself between the two hosts and said, "Gentlemen, we just started, come on. We need a little of Zach's flare *and* Tyler's science. I can set up shots for both of you. You know that, no need to argue."

Zach glared at the interloper. "Scooter, you're one of the best camera men in the business. I respect you. But this is my show and you need to be careful what you put yourself in the middle of."

Scooter Martin smiled back at him. "Zach, we do this every time, and in the end we do both shots and it makes for a better show. I have it covered, don't worry about it."

Zach scrapped a chair from a nearby table across the floor a few feet, then sat out in the open. He proceeded to fold his arms and sulk. "We start shooting tonight. The script better feature the shots I want." Then he rose and left.

Scooter turned to me. "Sorry about that. Zach is young. He can be, um, difficult at times. But this is par for the course. Everything is on schedule and the script writers will draft up the episode today based on what the co-hosts want after seeing the place. We'll finish unloading the gear now to be ready for setup and shooting tonight.

I asked, "Is there anything we need to do or be aware of?

Scooter went on. "No, And we won't bother you, not too much. We'll take care of everything and this place will become famous."

I glared at Scooter and said, "That's what I'm afraid of."

Chapter Two

The Potter's Mill gossip machine went into action. To be fair, this time the gossip machine had help in the form of a billboard on the side of the huge trailer parked in front of my pub. So the news was out, and as predicted by Piper, everyone did indeed want to be a guest at The Grumpy Chicken. For the first time ever, I had to keep a waiting list for seats at the bar and tables in the dining room. It was like a big city hot spot; there was even a line out front and Guardrail volunteered as a temporary bouncer to keep things calm and organized out on the sidewalk. We finished the day with one of the best single day sales total in the history of the pub. And we did it all while television producers prowled around my pub with writers, and an entire crew moved crate after crate into the dining room. It was fair to say it was a long day.

After we closed at eleven o'clock, I sat at a table and ate a late dinner. I watched the television crew work and saw they moved fast, unpacking the crates with precision. They knew what they were doing. One of the crew, an attractive young woman in her late twenties, sat down with me. She was definitely from Hollywood; she wore designer jeans and had on a nice diamond tennis bracelet. "Hello. My name is Denise Anderson. I'm one of the sound crew but I also do some special effects."

I squinted at her. "What does a TV show like this need a special effects person for?"

She leaned in a little to me. "Can you keep a secret?" I nodded yes. "Zach likes to play practical jokes. And we need to spice things up sometimes to make the show more interesting. So sometimes we add a little extra with special effects. Not too much and it's why I mostly work with the sound crew."

"Is that legal?"

Denise laughed then replied. "Legal, sure. Ethical, not really. But reality TV does it all the time. So it's normal believe it or not."

"My world isn't shattered, but it's a little surprising."

Denise smiled. "I'm not used to dealing with level headed, honest spectators while working on this show. Most just babble some nonsense till they finally get around to asking for Zach's autograph. You're a nice change of pace. Let me know if you need anything."

I paused at her sincerity. "That's nice of you. Really. You're the first one associated with this circus to realize there is more to life than the next camera shot."

She smiled and waggled her finger at me. "Don't say that to Zach! His world *is* the next shot. And thanks for the compliment, by the way. We can talk later and you can tell me what you think of the shoot tonight. We'll just get set up and do some establishing shots. Nothing fancy and we won't start the more interesting stuff till tomorrow night. So it should go nice and smooth tonight."

I nodded to her and sighed. "I hope so. See ya around then."

Denise went to work and I watched as the crew leapt into action. To be honest, I was most impressed with how boring it all was. Lots of waiting around and the cameras did not roll very much. It was lots of preparation for a few minutes of footage. And just like that, the first night was over, so I went upstairs to join Dad in the apartment and get some sleep.

***

Business the second day with the big truck parked out front went the same as the first. People lined up and we even needed to ask Piper and Ida to pitch in to work tables. Guardrail again worked the line out front while Dog Breath and Digger helped Bones in the kitchen. The boys had surrendered their prized bar stools, well rented them to be accurate. And Dad needed to work the bar with Dixie, a rare site. Apparently, people really want to be part of this three ring circus.

Lily and Edith held court at their regular table telling their tale a dozen times to anyone who would listen. When I passed their table, I heard the two elderly sisters describing their not so harrowing story of how they directed traffic out on Main Street, while cops captured a murderer. It was welcome background noise and kind of funny to listen to them talk about riding on the back of Dog and Guardrail's motorcycles. We had bonded as a team when we recently chased down the murder suspects together. So it was fitting to have the whole gang present during the television shoot to let off some steam together. And yes, two seventy year old spinsters who direct traffic and ride shotgun on motorcycles are part of our team.

Myself, I was a bit nervous. Last night was the first time I witnessed a television show being made and I wished it was not inside the pub. I was surprised with how many people were needed to make it happen. The Grumpy Chicken felt small all day with the large crowds, but after closing at eleven o'clock p.m. we were still crowded. We simply swapped our customers for a television crew. And then it was time to shoot a television series again.

The show made arrangements with Dad and me ahead of time. One of the things we asked for was a place to watch for Dad, Guardrail, Dog Breath, Digger, Edith, Lily, Piper, Ida, Dixie, Bones, and last but not least, me. The show went first class and had those special folding director chairs waiting for us all. Printed in bright white letters, the black cloth backs to the chairs declared "The Ghost Hounds." We were all giddy with the special treatment and we took our special access seats. Guardrail boomed. "It's show time."

"Hush. Come on now, they're getting ready to shoot." I didn't know if that was true. I looked over to Denise to see if they were in fact close to starting. But I saw her huddled with Zach. They whispered for a short time and then she handed him a small vial.

Stan, the director, then took center stage, which in this case was in my kitchen, right in front of the new, but now damaged whiteboard just outside my office. He raised his voice so all could hear. "Alright! Let's settle. This is a simple shot in front of this whiteboard. Zach and Tyler will discuss the weird writing and damage that was reported to appear on it last week. Cecil will examine the slight dent that is still there and write on the board trying to recreate or cause something to happen. Then we do some quick EMF and infrared tests to see if there are signs of the supernatural. Real simple, straightforward shot. Let's get it done." He clapped, and so did everyone else. I thought it was kind of odd they clapped for themselves, but it was obviously their sign to get to work.

Zach, Cecil, and Tyler took up position in front of the cameras at the whiteboard. The director yelled action, and then they did pretty much what the director said. At one point, the scene focused on Cecil showing the shallow dent in the whiteboard and he wrote something on it. I saw Zach, who was now out of the shot, take out the vile Denise gave him and turn his back to us.

A few moments later, the camera came back to Zach and things took a bizarre turn. A bright orange foam started to ooze from his mouth and nose. Then he grabbed at his throat, screaming, "The chicken ghost has me. It is trying to com...mun...icate with me. The chick... ach.. aaaaaaa..." The sounds eventually stopped and his face turned blue. After a few minutes of people trying to help him by patting him on the back, he fell to the floor.

Denise dropped her boom microphone and moved quickly to Zach. She scolded him. "Alright. That's enough Zach. Get up. You've had your fun." Tyler and Cecil had stepped aside and ignored the scene, seemingly not surprised by an apparent prank. But Zach didn't move. Denise continued. "Come on you ham. That's enough."

Tyler suddenly realized something was wrong. He rushed over to Zach and got down on his knees next to his incapacitated co-host. He felt for a pulse and then screamed. "Call nine one one." Tyler started CPR and tried to perform mouth to mouth resuscitation. To everyone's horror. Tyler was also using his index finger, digging something out of

Zach's mouth. Five minutes of terror passed while we waited for the ambulance and watched Tyler continue to work on Zach. As the medics arrived and started to administer care, Tyler stood and stepped aside to let them do their job. Then he looked over to the director and said, "I think he's dead."

Denise started to cry. "It was harmless seltzer with food coloring. It was safe, how could it hurt him?" She sobbed a little, then went on. "He had to do a prank that looked real. The fool, he always had to do a stinking prank."

Tyler went to her and gave her a hug. "That foam in his mouth is solid. I was trying to dig something solid out of his mouth. That wasn't seltzer powder."

Denise looked at Tyler stunned. "I know it was seltzer. I filled the vial myself. And Zach and I kept the prank a secret. How could seltzer and food coloring turn solid and kill him?"

I couldn't keep quiet any longer. "Now that's the million dollar question, isn't it? I think we need to call the police. And we need to leave this area alone. This may now be a crime scene." I took out my cell phone and called the Sheriff. I knew this drill. Unfortunately, it was the second time in a week I called in a dead body to the Potter's Mill police.

Chapter Three

I called Sheriff Kelly Morrison on his cell phone. He answered after one ring. "Hello, Sheriff. This is Ginger."

"I saw your number so I knew it was you. What's so important you have to call me directly this late? The pub been invaded by Martians?" He chuckled a little at the thought.

"I can't believe I have to call this in to you, but we have a dead TV host lying on the kitchen floor here at the Chicken."

The Sheriff was silent for a moment, then responded. "If this is a joke… Did Deputy Wise put you up to this?"

"No. I wish I didn't have to make this call, but a show host just choked on some orange gunk, turned blue, and fell dead on my floor."

"Twice in one week you find a dead body? What the heck is going on?"

"Actually, I didn't find the body this time. But I saw him choke to death in front of me."

"I'll be right there. Keep everyone away from the crime scene till I get there."

"Will do. I know the drill." I heard the phone click off.

I turned to the director. "The Sheriff says we need to keep everyone away from the scene and that he will be here in a few minutes."

After a couple of minutes, I heard the siren a ways down Main Street. It's wail continued to grow louder for the next couple of minutes until it was right out front of The Grumpy Chicken. Dad unlocked the front entrance to let Sheriff Morrison in and he came running in through the open door into the dining room.

The Sheriff addressed a medic near the entrance as he came in. "What's the status?"

The medic looked at him with a blank face. "You serious? He's dead. Go see for yourself." The medic pointed to the swinging door and the Sheriff strode over to the kitchen entrance. He went in to view the body on the ground, which was now covered with a white table cloth.

Kelly shook his head no. "Not again." Then he moved to the crime scene and began isolating the area, all the while looking for clues.

Deputy Mae Owens and Deputy Leonard Wise showed up shortly after the Sheriff. They corralled everyone into the dining room, out of the kitchen, which was now a potential crime scene. They sprinkled us around the dining area to separate and prevent us from talking to each other. The number of people present when Zach choked was large and the police had their work cut out for them.

The Sheriff took one of the dining tables and set it off to one side of the room, isolating it. Then he started bringing people over individually to interview them. He began the interviews with Denise Anderson, the girl who handed Zach Black the vial of powder. It seemed like a logical place to start. Deputy Wise and Owens finished roping off the kitchen area where Zach choked and then they looked for evidence.

As far as I could see, the list of clues was short. But I did know Zach and Tyler argued, which Scooter indicated happened often. Denise gave Zach the vial of powder. I also saw Zach take the vial out and it appeared that he snorted it, but his back was to us so I didn't actually see it inhaled. However, it was likely he did. Then the weird orange foam appeared and a few minutes or so after that his face started to turn blue. But that was the extent of the evidence I could see. This was nothing like the murder scene I observed last week.

With so many people in the pub, I would never believe it could be so quiet. But it was. Edith finally broke the silence and said. "Dear, I was glad when you invited us to this and it was one heck of a show, for sure. But now I'm not so certain we want to be here."

I sighed a little. "I'm sorry, Edith. But I don't think you can leave. The Sheriff made it clear he wants to speak with everyone that saw the incident. And that includes us."

Lily pouted. "Oh pish posh. Why can't we leave? We're two old ladies that were just sitting here minding our own business."

"I know. But it's what the police have to do. We just have to wait."

Deputy Owens, my Aunt Mae, let us talk a little then said, "I'm really sorry, but it would be best if you didn't talk right now. You know, to let the Sheriff do his job."

I knew the police didn't want us to talk until they debriefed everyone. So we waited – in silence. At about four o'clock in the morning, the Sheriff had completed interviews with Tyler, Cecil, Denise, the director Stan, Scooter the cameraman, and two other television crew members that had direct contact with Zach. I figured out that Sheriff Kelly was interviewing in a particular order, starting with those most likely to have access to the vial of powder down to those not probable. It was smart and he had completed interviews with the most likely suspects based on access to the powder.

After that, the Sheriff rose to address the mass of people waiting in my dining room. "Thank you everyone for your patience. I think we're done for tonight and I am going to let you go back to The Fluffy Pillow and get some sleep. But I'm afraid I have to ask you to not leave town for now and avoid discussing this with anyone, even among yourselves.

I still have interviews to complete with your crew, and details and statements to corroborate. In effect, you are being placed under house arrest. I need to ask you to remain in the B&B for now." I guess the Sheriff decided the unlikely suspects could wait and he was tired.

The crew replied in unison. "Ahhh."

Kelly shied back a little. "I know. But it looks like we had a terrible accident – or maybe even a suicide or murder. I need to be able to interview everyone and confirm the information I gather before I can let you leave. Deputy Wise has been booked into The Fluffy Pillow with you and he will be there to make sure you comply with our request."

Deputy Owens and Deputy Wise were now in the kitchen. They had another crime scene to investigate and were not about to let anyone contaminate it or mess with any clues. Meanwhile, The Ghost Hounds crew and staff headed out of The Grumpy Chicken to make the short walk over to The Fluffy Pillow.

**

After only a couple of hours sleep, the Sheriff was up and back to it at nine a.m.. He made his way over to The Fluffy Pillow and I watched him set up an area within the bed and breakfast lobby to complete his interviews. Since we were witnesses that also needed to be questioned, the gang and I were there waiting as requested by Sheriff Morrison.

As his second interview of the morning started,

Cecil, the slightly pudgy and clumsy co-host, barged into the questioning of a teleprompter operator and started rambling. "Why are you focusing on us? That pub owner, Tom, set this all up. He's the one who brought us out here to chase that ridiculous story about a ghost chicken. Plus we paid him good money for the rights to shoot there. Now he stands to make out since his bar is the place where Zach died. Every fan of the show will flock to his place now. The pub owner is the only one to profit from all this. He's the one you should be talking to."

The Sheriff kept his cool and responded, "What's your name again?"

"Cecil."

Sheriff Morrison stood and went eyeball to eyeball with Cecil. "Yeah, that's right, I remember now. Cecil, I have a job to do in order to figure out if all this was a horrible accident or not. If not, then it's possible Zach committed suicide or maybe someone murdered him. I know it seems inconvenient to you, but I'm trying to make sure we do our job so that in case it *isn't* an accident, we find the person responsible for your co-host's death. I would think you would want that too and a little patience is not much to ask in order to help us."

Cecil just stared back in response. He then repeated, "You need to interview the pub owner too!" Then he stormed back to his room.

I spoke to the Sheriff. "It seems lack of sleep and a bizarre murder are too much for a ghost hunter."

The Sheriff looked over to me sideways. "Who said it was a murder. It's a *potential* murder. There's a difference."

"I'm sorry. I should have said bizarre death." I knew how serious the Sheriff was with this type of work and I was actually a little embarrassed for choosing my words poorly.

And then in an incredible example of bad timing, my father came sauntering into the B&B to join us. Seems Cecil would get his request. Tom O'Mallory was on the list of people to interview. Everyone stared at my father when he entered, causing him to stop. He looked around then said to no one in particular, "What?"

I patted a seat next to me and replied. "Dad, come sit here with me. I need to talk to you."

Dad mumbled something I couldn't understand and he took the seat. I put my arm around him. "The Sheriff is going to ask you some questions. You need to answer them and not be difficult. Dad, it's important to be honest and not say more than you have to."

"Sweetie, why in the world are you telling me this? I know how to talk with the Sheriff."

I smiled at Dad, trying to not let him see I was concerned. "It's complicated. One of the hosts, Cecil, just told the Sheriff you might be someone of interest. You know, since you arranged for them to come out here and shoot."

Dad just folded his arms and snorted. I could see he was mulling over what I'd just told him.

Chapter Four

It was now mid-afternoon and after the interviews were done, I asked the gang to assemble back at the chicken. I was concerned Cecil called out my father and made some not so veiled accusations. As I waited in my office for the gang to arrive, Ida strolled into the office and took her seat, well actually it was my seat, behind the desk. Piper came in not far behind her and sat on one of the two pub chairs I keep in the office.

I asked, "Is everyone else coming?"

Piper answered, "Yep, they just wanted to freshen up or get something to eat or drink first. It was a long drawn out interview process and everyone is tired but they should be here in a few minutes."

"In the meantime, I did want to talk with the two of you alone. Dad was mentioned to the Sheriff by Cecil as a potential suspect because he made the arrangements with the producers and was paid. Also, my kitchen is shut down because a large portion of it may be a crime scene. So I think the best way to help Dad and get my kitchen back is to find out who really did this, fast! For now, let's leave the hack shack set up in my office here, to investigate the death of Zach Black."

Ida looked a little surprised. "Sure, it's more fun to work here with everyone. And it's already up and running."

Piper added, "The gang is back in action?"

Ida said, "Team PMF that is!"

Both Piper and me moaned. "Nooo! That sounds awful."

The door was open and Dixie wandered in. "So what's new?"

Ida was quickest to respond. "We're back in the investigation business. We need to help figure this latest incident out to help Tom and get your kitchen back."

Dixie made an odd whistling noise. "Bull shots! That's a stretch. There is no way Tom had anything to do with this. And I would like to have the kitchen back, customers drink more when they have hot food to eat."

I grinned. "That's one of your better non-curse swear word inventions. Our swear jar is going to be hard to fill if you keep that up. And yes it is a real stretch to accuse Dad, but he is not going to help things with his charming personality. And I need my kitchen open to make ends meet. So it's best if we help figure out who did it, fast." I spun to face the desk and my tone may have been a tad sarcastic. "And Ida, thanks for being so understanding about how I wanted to talk to you alone so no one else would know what we're up to."

Ida stared at me like I caught her with a hand in the

cash register. "What? I just assumed everyone would know about it. Lots of other people heard Cecil down at The Fluffy Pillow and everybody knows your kitchen is closed and that you'll want it back."

Dixie cleared her throat. "Well, that's actually why I'm here. Beth is out in the bar talking about it."

I rolled my eyes. "I better go see what nonsense Beth is spreading. Son of a muddler! I don't need this now." Beth is our resident gossip monger. She's like radar...she can spot tales of slander a mile away. The doorway then darkened. It was the big frame of Guardrail, closely followed by Dog Breath and Digger.

Guardrail had a scowl on his face. "You know I have a business to run too, don't you Ginger?"

I looked at him not sure if it was the lack of sleep or the interview that made him sour. It was not like him and I replied, "I know, but things right now are a little abnormal, to say the least. I'm hoping we can put our team into action to find the real reason Zach died."

"You better. If you listen to Beth Givens, Tom is convicted and awaiting sentencing." Digger responded.

I tilted my head back in a sort of surrender. "Alright! I thought we would have a little time to work things out. But I can't have my father getting caught up in this mess. We need to figure this out fast. It would seem our team is back up and running."

Dog lit up. "The Grumpy Gumshoes are back in action!"

I pointed at him. "Mr. Dog Breath, we never agreed to a name. But we did do good work. So, if we can find the answer to how that weird powder got into Zach's nose and mouth, we'll clear Tom of all suspicion and I get my kitchen back."

"I'm not working any traffic duty again!" Guardrail chirped

Digger complained, "Please let there be no cats I hope? I hate cats."

Dog raised his voice, "It's a hit man ghost to prevent The Ghost Hounds from finding proof that the supernatural really exists." In response, everyone in the room looked at him like he grew two additional heads. He responded, "What? I was right last time. Trust me."

Guardrail broke into laughter. "Dog, some days I really worry about you."

Unlike the boys, I tried to focus on the problems at hand. "Our first move should be to learn about Denise and Tyler. I think those two had the most interaction with Zach. Denise gave him the vial and Tyler openly argued with him right in front of us."

Ida added, "I agree, but what about the other host, that Cecil. It's odd he would accuse Tom like he did. I say we look at him too. That Zach was a looker, but he seemed difficult to work with, and if Tyler was at odds with him, Cecil might be too."

I nodded. "That makes sense. Can you and Piper get that going, Ida?"

Ida shrugged. "Sure. You know we can."

Edith and Lily finally appeared and walked in on our planning session. Edith said, "Well, what's going on here? If I didn't know better, I would say the gang is back at work."

Dog blurted out, "We are!"

Lily looked at Edith with a broad smile. "You think we'll get to ride on the back of the hogs again?"

Edith smiled back. "One can only hope. I so love the roar of a motorcycle engine and the open road. The wind in my hair feels so good."

Guardrail hung his head at the two over seventy spinster sisters talking about his motorcycle. Then I heard Bones outside the office yell, "Hey boss, come look at this!"

I made my way out of the office and over to the order counter in the kitchen. I asked Bones, "Where did you find this?"

Bones pointed. "It was in the bin for bills of lading. I could tell it wasn't something that belonged in that pile the minute I saw it. The police must have missed it."

Dad had wandered over to see what was going on. "That's my boy. Not so smart with the girls, but you know your work. Spotted something out of place right off."

I held out my hand. "Let me have a look." Bones handed me the script. What caught my eye was all the red ink. And when I scanned the page, I saw this was the page for the whiteboard scene. The very scene where Zach choked to death. I also noticed it belonged to one of the camera people. "This is Scooter Martin's copy. And we saw him splitting up the argument between Zach and Tyler. Looking at this page, seems Zach was pretty hard on Scooter."

Bones scratched his head. "I don't know about all that, but glad it means something to ya."

"Thanks, Bones."

I took the script back to the office. The boys were teasing Ida, something about her lack of understanding on the finer points of betting. I eyed the boys. "I have said this before, but just to confirm, there's to be no gambling inside the Chicken."

Dog looked up. "Who? Us?"

I growled and frowned at the boys. "Yes, you." Then I held up the script. "Look at this. It's Scooter's copy and it seems Zach asked for all kinds of revisions. Maybe in retaliation for Scooter breaking up the spat Zach had with Tyler?"

Ida asked, "Are you saying we should put Scooter on the suspect list?"

I paused. "Yeah, I am. Zach snarled at Scooter after he broke up the squabble with Tyler. Scooter may have more to his story. And remember, he said this type of thing happened all the time with Zach. I don't think those two are friends."

Piper chuckled. "I don't think Zach has many friends to be honest. He was kind of a pill. Why do all the pretty ones have such awful personalities."

I looked at Piper for a moment. "That's true, and it's what scares me right now. I think everyone on that crew has to be a suspect to be honest. I sensed no one liked Zach."

Guardrail added, "I agree. I thought the guy was a twit."

Ida brought things back to her own domain. "So what are you saying? We need to do background checks on all of the crew?"

I sighed. "Maybe. It's interesting. I think the Sheriff had a similar thought process. I noticed that he interviewed the most likely suspects last night. Before they could talk to anyone or do something to destroy evidence. And that included Stan the director, Cecil, Tyler, Denise, Scooter and two other crew members I don't know. For now I think we have to assume that is our tier one suspect list."

Ida jumped in. "I can check them all. Do we have

names for the other two crew members?"

I turned to Lily and Edith. "Ladies, you think you can use your charms to find the names for those two crew members interviewed by the Sheriff last night?"

Lily beamed. "Of course, sweetie, we're part of the gang and quite resourceful."

"Good." I spun back to Ida. "Get going on everyone else on the tier one list while Lily and Edith chase down those last two names. Also, what happened to Zach? What kind of powder could do that to someone? And who could get that kind of thing? I kept asking myself those questions all day while I waited over at the B&B to be interviewed."

Piper noted, "Tyler said he was digging something solid out of Zach's mouth. I found that so gross! But it was also odd, so I wondered what kind of material could do that."

Digger spoke up. "Well, it's kind of obvious then. How do we find out what could have done that to a man? And who would know how to get something like that?"

I added, "I don't know, Digger, but we have to figure it out. And there is one more thing. It seems like either Denise put a killer powder in the vial, or she put harmless seltzer in the vial like she said. So the big question is, did Denise do it, or did someone change out the powder in the vial?"

Piper's eyes grew wide. "How in the blazes are we going to find that out?"

I replied, "I didn't say it was going to be easy."

***

Edith and Lily returned about an hour later with the two names of a boom operator and a grip. So Ida added Cory Lynch and Kenny White to our suspect list.

Meanwhile, our food service was out of commission, meaning I was not as busy as usual. The area in front of the whiteboard was roped off, eliminating a large portion of my kitchen, and I could not cook food. That was bad for business. I was a little surprised that I was still allowed to use my office, which is off the kitchen.

But fortunately, I could still sell drinks and continue to make some money until all this all blew over. So, Dixie was working the bar with Bones' help. Technically, Bones was underage to be working in the bar area, but in small towns sometimes you just need to do what you have to do and the law cuts you some slack.

I pondered the dilemma and our suspect list. Denise, Tyler, Cecil, Stan, and Scooter were most likely. But the Sheriff did interview two additional crew members that night, Cory and Kenny. I was not sure why. From what I could see they did not have much access to Zach. It was likely the Sheriff had moved on to his second level suspects to complete as many interviews the night of the incident, and Cory and Kenny were just the first two he picked. But it was easy enough for Ida to send out her creepy little web crawlers and get background information on all seven of them.

I had bigger questions that needed answers. How was I going to find out about the bizarre cause of death? Where would I look for someone who would know enough about chemistry to tell me what kind of powder could cause a solid to form inside the respiratory system and choke a person to death? And who put the deadly powder in the vial? That last question was so simple and straightforward. But finding an answer to it might be the hardest.

Chapter Five

Later that afternoon, The Ghost Hounds crew assembled at the big rig parked in front of the Grumpy Chicken. The TV crew was working to get ready for a shoot on the Main Street sidewalk. We were all surprised to see them working and the gang assembled with them on the sidewalk to watch.

I asked Tyler, "What are you guys doing? Your co-host just died and you are supposed to be under house arrest?"

Tyler replied, "No, correction. We were asked not to leave town and we're complying. But your Sheriff was not so trusting and asked Cecil, Denise, Scooter and me to wear ankle bracelets to make sure we complied." Tyler lifted his pants leg to reveal the bulky, black plastic wrapped around his ankle.

Denise jumped in. "Not so fashionable is it. I guess I won't be wearing shorts for a while. And it clashes with my Calvin jeans!" She lifted her pant's leg just like Tyler had and revealed her ankle bracelet.

I was surprised. "I didn't know Potter's Mill had those things."

Cecil grumbled. "You don't. State police provided them. And good thing, your Sheriff Wise had no idea how to install these things on us. Talk about country bumpkins."

Tyler jumped on Cecil. "Quiet, you idiot. Small town life is different. But it doesn't mean the people are bumpkins."

Denise twirled her hair. "What does bumpkin mean anyway?"

Tyler eyed her, trying to determine if she was serious. "You know, a local, but simple in the head."

Denise raised her eyebrows. "Oh! Cecil, that's' not nice. And Deputy Wise was so nice to us. He was worried about messing it up, too. Said the Sheriff would make him shovel horse stalls if he did."

I interrupted. "That's true, the Sheriff loves those police horses and anyone who is in the dog house with him gets mucking duty. But more important, how can you shoot so soon after Zach's death?"

Cecil replied, "It's what we do. Zach would want it and we need to get to work, get back to normal."

Tyler commented, "Cecil, Zach is dead and I'm not sure things will ever be normal again. But you're right about one thing. We should get back to shooting to honor the hard work Zach put into this."

Stan the director stood in the center of the TV crew and used a megaphone. "We're going to get some memorial words from Tyler and Cecil in front of the pub. While we are outside, we can also interview the store owner next door. She's agreed to an interview on the sidewalk out front and owns a new age shop. And she says she is psychic. So she may have some interesting stories to share with us. After that, I'm hoping we will have time then to go back into the pub and film shots of Cecil and Tyler showing off the new infrared camera. And I want all of you watching and making sure the ankle monitors on Cecil and Tyler are not visible in any shot. Alright, I want you on your A game and let's make some magic." As before, they all clapped and went to work.

The memorial shot in front of the pub happened fast. Cecil and Tyler said some short but kind words about Zach, but not surprisingly it did not feel warm or friendly.

Then the crew reset outside of Star's store and she came out to be interviewed. She had on a pretty yellow dress and her hair was neatly coiffed. I was not used to seeing her with make-up and she looked different.

The director yelled action and Tyler started. "You're located next door to a pub that is reported to be haunted by a dead chicken. You own a new age store and are a medium. Have you seen anything that indicates a ghost chicken occupies the pub?"

Star touched her hair and I think she blushed. "Well, yes. It's strange, but at times I get this out of body feeling. I freeze and cannot see clearly. It is like being lost in a dense fog. It doesn't happen all that often. But every time it does, there are stories from the pub about hearing the chicken squawk or something strange."

Cecil said, "Can you explain what the fog looked like."

Star looked at him puzzled. "It's fog. It's white and blank."

Tyler sighed. "Well, when it has happened, Star, have you heard anything?"

She thought a moment. "Just last week I went into the fog and I thought I heard what sounded like a chicken, but saying evil."

My heart froze when I heard her say that. The pub was full when it happened and everyone heard it. Guardrail leaned over to me and whispered. "Now that's spooky. She wasn't there, how could she know that?"

I answered. "Hush. Let's not complicate things right now. We need to stay focused on figuring out how Zach died."

Piper was next to me and must have heard us because she added, "Guardrail is right! How could she know that? Look, I got goosebumps."

I hushed them both. I was afraid of what else Star might tell them. But the sidewalk interview with her finished and before I knew it the crew was in my dining room again. It was a little after dinner time and the dining room was empty. A sad sight for my tired eyes. But it made it easy for the many people involved with the television show to move in early and do some work.

Cameras were mounted and wires were run across the floor everywhere. Eventually Tyler and Cecil took their position and I saw a handheld device. The bright yellow color was hard to miss in Tyler's hands and they were intently hovering over it, chatting.

Tyler said, "This one records real time video. And it measures temperatures of everything in the frame very accurately. It was expensive, but worth it."

Cecil asked, "How are you going to use it?"

"To scan areas. We can record ninety minutes of video with this baby. So I can scan each area where we shoot. It only takes a few minutes to scan a large area."

Cecil giggled, taking the camera to look at it more closely. "Cool. I can't wait to see what it captures."

"Well, it would be better if it were late at night when the spirits were more active. But this will be a good test drive."

At that point, the director yelled and Cecil and Tyler went into TV host mode. They spoke different when in front of the camera and Tyler did most of the talking. He was explaining the new piece of equipment and why an infrared camera helps with hunting ghosts. "When spirits appear, the temperature falls. It gets cold. This camera sees temperature, and displays that data in a color map of the image. Red and yellow are hot, blue and green are cold."

Tyler then scanned a wall in the dining room followed by the director yelling cut.

Then a familiar voice shot through the space. It was Guardrail sitting on his usual bar stool drinking a beer. He addressed Stan the director. "You're looking in the wrong spot. You need to scan under this bar stool right here. I saw six or seven ghost mice right here not too long ago."

The director looked at Cecil and Tyler but didn't say a thing. In response Tyler said, "Sure we can do it. It's easy to scan with the infrared camera. It'll be harder for you to move the cameras, which isn't too hard either. But moving that big guy off his stool, that might be another thing. I'm not doing it."

The director bellowed, "Let's reset near the bar. You heard the big guy at the bar, that's our next shot."

It took about twenty minutes, but eventually they talked Guardrail into surrendering his stool and they reset to shoot there. The director yelled action again, and to my amazement, we had "professionals" looking under Guardrail's bar stool for ghost mice. When they finished, it was Dog Breath that spoke first. "Hey, what are you going to say when they show there's nothing under your stool."

"Maybe they did find something. We'll just have to wait and see. But I can tell you for sure, they're not going to find a hit man ghost." Guardrail looked down at Dog Breath as he spoke.

Dog took a sip of his beer and never looked up. Just after that he said into his mug, "I was right last time."

Tyler had a laptop setup on one of my dining room tables and he took an SD card out of the infrared camera, then put it into the computer. He fired up the media player and watched the video he captured. The laptop was also hooked up to a monitor so the crew could watch. I had a good view, too. We watched in the same order as they were shot, viewing the scan of the dining room wall first. Tyler started the video and put it on fast forward, just enough to quickly scan the video but still slow enough to see everything just fine. While the pictures were colorful and pretty, there was nothing unusual to see.

Then he opened the file from the scan under Guardrail's stool. Again he put it on fast forward and we all watched. About half way through, Tyler paused the video and popped up like a jack-in-the-box, knocking his chair over. I saw it too. It looked like four small, blue pong balls moving along the base of the bar. Tyler rewound, or I guess with digital video there is no tape to rewind, so he reversed the video and replayed it. This time in slow motion. He said, "There's definitely something there. The blue color indicates something real cold. There were four mice sized anomalies under that stool. But we have to be careful not to jump to conclusions."

Guardrail shrieked like a little girl. "I'm not sitting

there anymore. No way. Dog, switch with me!"

Dog shook his head and laughed. "I don't think so. You've sat there for years and it has worked just fine. I'm not going to mess with the seating order now."

Digger burped, then added, "You have pets. That's nice Guardrail. Why would you want to move?"

The big man's voice went up a few octaves. "Because there are real ghost mice under my feet. I can't sit there drinking beer knowing that."

Dog shot back, "Well, maybe they don't like you either."

Tyler spoke again. "Gentlemen. If I can break up this little meeting, the four spots are small. They could be apparitions, but this building is old and they may just be some cold spots. I need to do a little more analysis. We were just trying out the camera and moving kind of fast. It will take a little more analysis to confirm that this was an apparition."

Guardrail spoke quickly. "Well, are you going to do the additional work now? I need to know if there are ghost mice under my bar stool."

Tyler rubbed his chin. "Let me look at the rest of this video first. We stopped when we saw these four spots, but there is more to the video. Let's have a look."

Tyler went back to the keyboard, plunked a few

keys and restarted the video. After a minute he popped up again, but this time he not only knocked the chair over, he was holding his head with both hands and exclaimed, "Holy moly. Now that's unusual."

We all saw it too and Dixie's voice rose from behind the bar. "What the fungus is that thing?"

Tyler answered, "I don't know." Then he flipped through this portion of the video frame by frame. Eventually he stopped on one frame with what appeared to be the clearest image of the anomaly.

I was mute. The image I saw was disturbing. But the most upsetting part of it was that the blue pattern this time was larger and shaped in such a way that it could only be a chicken. A chicken with a limp.

Chapter Six

The next morning I woke in my bed feeling groggy. I heard Dad in the apartment kitchen making coffee. I slept little and felt a headache trying to form. The creepy image from yesterday filled my thoughts and I knew this was going to be a problem. Everyone saw it and I was sure it would make it harder to stay focused on solving the mystery of Zach's death.

I rose, and studied my face in the mirror. I hated my brown eyes and they looked worse with signs of fatigue. Using makeup was never my strong suit and I didn't wear it too often. But today I used a little to try and hide the ugly black rings under my eyes. I detested my wavy, red hair too and it was a mess. I brushed it out and pulled it into a pony tail, tying it off with a fresh, white ribbon. Then I dressed and noticed the only good thing with this investigative work, I seemed to have lost a little weight and my jeans were a little looser. Yeah for the silver lining!

Dad yelled from the tiny apartment kitchen, "Ginger, I made some coffee. Come join me...have a mug with me. I want to talk with you about how we use this proof of the ghost chicken in the pub to help us make more money."

Just as I thought, the blue image that looked like the limping grumpy chicken's ghost was going to be distraction. I joined Dad and drank a couple of cups of Joe with him. He said, "What do you think about running some commercials? We can show that picture of the chicken those silly ghost hounds found."

"Dad, it's not a picture of the chicken. It's a blue

blob."

"Nonsense! You always want to explain our spirit clucker away."

"I just don't want to exaggerate anything, Dad. Look, I need to go check on something in my office. Figure out how we're going to pay the bills with a closed kitchen."

I finished the last dregs of coffee and kissed my father on the cheek. Then I headed down to my office to think and be alone. But when I got there I found a surprise. Ida was there working. "What are you doing here? Did you stay here last night? You're wearing the same clothes."

She looked at me puzzled and I think she blushed. "Yeah. That's it. I stayed here last night. Don't you know hackers keep odd hours sometimes? I was finding out a lot and didn't want to stop."

"Well, then. What did you find?"

Ida spun her laptop so I could better see her screen. "Look at this. I found it on Youtube." She hit the space bar and the video started.

I saw Zach and Cecil inside what looked like a child's bedroom. They were shooting a scene from the Ghost Hounds. Zach said, "Hey Cecil, this looks like it could be your bedroom."

Cecil scrunched his face and asked, "What? This is a little girl's room."

"Exactly. Just like I imagine your bedroom would be."

Cecil huffed and sprinted out of the shot. Ida sighed. "This an outtake from the show. I found dozens of them. Seems Zach was pretty hard on Cecil. And on camera. The show didn't air any of Zach's degrading behavior, but outtakes are all over Youtube. Zach did not treat Cecil very well."

"So, are you saying Cecil might have some motive to murder Zach?"

"Duh, yeah!"

I rolled my eyes. "I don't see that as being enough to want to kill someone. So keep your duhs in a jar."

"Oh don't be so sensitive. And look at this next video."

I complied with her request. This time I saw Zach humiliate Cecil in front of a girl I didn't recognize. "So Zach acted awful on other occasions, you already told me that."

"Yeah, but I also found an email from Cecil, about the girl in the video. Seems Cecil liked her and wanted a date with her, but it seems Zach pulled that stunt just to make sure Cecil would never get the chance."

"Well, that was mean."

Ida nodded. "Zach was a mean man. I also found that Zach had an affair with Scooter's wife. And it led to a divorce for Scooter. The court records tell of some nasty business between the two of them. Seems Zach has a pattern of being a womanizer and stealing other men's girlfriends or wives."

I rubbed the back of my neck. "Well that complicates things. I was thinking Denise had the best access to the vial. After all, she gave it to Zach. And I could tell Tyler harbors resentment for him. So I was thinking they were the two strongest suspects, but what you're telling me is, Scooter and Cecil might have more motive than we thought and might be prime candidates too."

"It's clear Zach was demeaning to other males and he wanted every woman for himself. I'm not an expert in the male universe… Hmm, maybe that's why a looker like me is still single?… Anyhoo, I do think Zach's behavior might cause some dangerous enemies."

"Ida, first, your humility is overwhelming and we can talk about why you're still single later. But second, you're right about the male ego thing. Men get so irrational when a woman is involved. And they do the most stupid things when jealous or humiliated."

"And get this, Denise once dated Zach. I found a bunch of emails that read like love letters. I'm not sure why they split up yet, but they did and the love emails stopped suddenly. And the few sent after that, let's say, they were not very friendly."

"Zach was just making friends everywhere." I

paused. "Seems you found a lot all of a sudden. Did you get lucky or something?"

"Yeah, sometimes you find things quick. Sometimes not. These Hollywood types try to stay private and are pretty good at it. But I figured out how they like to work. So a bit lucky I guess."

"Hmm. So he dated Denise. I guess I'm not surprised, she is a looker. But that means messing with men's egos was not enough for Zach. He invited a women's scorn, too. And you know what they say about a woman scorned?"

Ida chuckled a little. "Yeah, don't do it!"

I looked her square in the eye. "You were more right than you knew last night when you said we may have to investigate the whole crew. He was a real son of a biscuit."

"That is one way to put it. But the whole crew is going to take a ton of time to check. I still don't even know the names of all of them. Okay, if I'm hearing you right, Denise, Tyler, Cecil and Scooter are strong suspects. I notice Stan the director has not popped up in anything yet. As well as the crew members Kenny and Cory. It appears for now, we have four strong suspects. That sounds right to me and I can start more detailed background searches on all four."

"Okay. That sounds good. But keep your eyes open. I think we have to assume that it could still be anyone."

Piper entered the office and plunked down in a chair. "My head is killing me. I didn't sleep a wink after seeing that blue dollop last night."

I replied, "I don't think that's our biggest problem. Piper, how can we find out what kind of powder could kill a man like that?"

"The closest we have to a chemist in town is the pharmacist and Star."

I wrinkled my forehead. "Star?"

Piper shrugged. "Yeah. She knows about some herbs and potions I think. She even sells some. You know that. Remember she was telling you she had some sort of powder to help you with those bad headaches when you were going through your divorce?"

"I remember now. And she seemed to know a little about the chemistry of how it worked. You're right."

Piper raised her eyebrows. "You want to go have a visit with her? See if she knows anything about a powder that could swell and become solid enough to choke a person to death?"

"I sure do. And after that, we should visit the pharmacy counter at the general store and inquire there as well. I want to know what kind of powder could do something like this. And how hard it would be to obtain."

***

So, there we were knocking on the front door of the new age store just before Star opened for business. She unlocked the door and could not hide the surprise on her face. "What are you ladies doing here so early?"

I answered, "We would like to have a word with you."

She giggled a little. "Okay? Well, that sounds almost official."

Piper responded, "In a way it is. We have lots of questions about the recent accident and you might be able to help us with some of them."

"Sure, come on in." Star opened the door all the way as she spoke and held her hand out, inviting us in. We entered, then she closed the door and led us into the store.

We followed and saw shelves filled with odd trinkets and books. Eventually, we took seats at a round table covered with a ruby red cloth in the middle of the store. On it sat a crystal ball and what I think were tarot-cards. Star spoke first. "I am so happy to have you here. We should do a reading sometime."

I answered. "That will have to wait. I need to know if you are aware of any kind of powder that would swell and become solid in a person's nasal cavities. Enough to choke them to death."

Star put her hands down gently on the table. "I

wondered the same thing. So, I consulted some tea leaves last night to see what they would tell. But it was not much. And then I remembered back to when I studied magic, to learn how the fake psychics out there pull off some their tricks."

"You studied magic?" Piper asked.

"Of course. I study lots of things. And I remember one book talked about a powder that could make water turn solid. It was used by magicians to create the illusion of water disappearing. The magicians call it slush powder, I think."

Piper interrupted. "So could it kill a man if it was snorted?"

"It actually did on one occasion. I remembered reading that obscure magician's reference in the book because I also saw a TV show not too long ago where two crooks were robbing a magician. They found some slush powder and thought it was cocaine. They snorted it and they died, very similar to Zach."

Piper leaned on the table. "So do you remember what show it was?"

"Of course, 101 Unique Deaths."

I sat up straight, ready to leave. "Thanks Star. That's real helpful. By the way, are you still able to play this Friday night? I can only sell drinks right now and may hold a special event to highlight your music. You know, make it more of a night club experience."

"I love that. Maybe you could create a makeshift dance floor for the event? I would like to see people dancing to my music."

"That'll be easy. I'll just move the dining room tables. No one is eating at them now."

Star smiled and reached out to touch my hand. "You're so sweet. And I am so glad you came by today. And really, I would love to do a reading for you. Your aura is unparalleled."

"Thanks for the help Star. But I need to take a rain check on that reading. We have a lot of work to do now. I need to get my kitchen back open and can't afford to waste any time."

"I understand. See ya around. Thanks for coming by."

I stood. "Thank you for the information. Bye for now."

We left and canceled our trip to the pharmacy counter. We instead headed straight for The Grumpy Chicken. Television shows seemed to be a major part of my life all of a sudden and I needed to know more about 101 Unique Deaths. At least one episode in particular.

Piper and I returned to the office to find Ida chatting with Lily and Edith. As we came in, I heard Ida say, "The crew was saying the image was so unusual and interesting. They want to use a Ouija board tonight to try and communicate with the spirits."

Edith said, "Oh my, that's so interesting. I remember those boards from when we were kids. I didn't think anyone took them serious."

Ida shook her head and replied, "Well the older guy, Tyler, agrees with you. He argued with the director and made the case it was only a toy with no scientific value. But Stan chewed out Tyler for being difficult and told him that the board was going to be used – to the delight of the chubby host, Cecil."

I interrupted. "Ladies, the Ouija board is an interesting topic, but I need to look at something a little different if we can."

Lily shifted in her seat and said, "Sweetie, you'll never get another man if you keep commandeering conversations."

"I'm not looking for a man right now, I want my kitchen back and I want strangers that don't know my father to stop making accusations. Ida, can you find a particular episode from the TV show, 101 Unique Deaths?"

"Of course, what episode you want?

"The one where two thieves die because they snorted a magician's powder they robbed thinking it was cocaine. They both died in a similar manner to Zach."

"So would you call that episode Thugs N Drugs?"

I glared back at her and replied, "That's not funny. Please find the episode so we can learn about it."

"You don't have to be so bossy!"

"I said please."

And as if she wanted to show off, in what seemed like a few seconds she spun her screen for all to see and played the episode on her laptop. It showed exactly what Star described. The powder was indeed called slush powder and it killed in the same manner as we witnessed with Zach, with one exception. The color of the solid foam that killed the two thieves was white, not orange.

Chapter Seven

Deputy Mae Owens worked on the Potter's Mill police force for twenty plus years, but she has been my aunt her entire life. I recently realized how I viewed her simply as my aunt, until last week when I saw her in action as a police officer. She was impressive and good at it. Aunt Mae came into the pub wearing her campaign hat and I knew that meant she was working on something serious. I was behind the bar and she moved over to meet me. Aunt Mae sat down on one of the bar stools. "Ginger, sweetie, how are you doing? The place looks strange with no one eating in the dining room. I guess the food is more a part of this place than I thought."

I walked out from behind the bar and over to her as she talked, then gave her a hug. "Auntie, glad you came by. But as you noted, you're not going to get any lunch here today."

Mae took her hat off and set it on the bar. "I'm not here for the food. I wanted to talk to you. Maybe you can help me with some questions I have. You know, since you saw the accident in your kitchen?"

"Sure, whatever you need."

Mae thought for a moment, then asked, "We found out what the substance in the victim's nasal passages was..."

"Slush powder!"

Mae looked puzzled, "Well, the lab said sodium polyacrylate. But they did say it had some slang names too."

"It's used by magicians. And it's the same thing as that sodium poly thing. Ida looked it up for me."

"And tell me sweetie, how did you find this out?"

"Just some luck, I guess. Star knew of a TV show that showed how two crooks were killed in a similar manner."

"What?"

"They were thieves, robbing a magician. They found his slush powder when they robbed him. The performer used it to make it look like water disappeared. But the crooks thought it was cocaine and they snorted it, dying in a way very similar to what we saw with Zach Black."

Mae tilted her head back and chuckled. "You were faster then the state labs I think. That's actually impressive sweetie. But what did I tell you about interfering with police business?"

"It's dangerous, don't do it."

"Right! So what part of that is hard to understand?"

"The part where I am losing sales because my kitchen is closed. I need this matter resolved and my kitchen reopened."

Mae pinched her lips. "I'm sure that's a problem

for you, dear. I know your margins are thin and the food business helps to make ends meet. But I don't want you getting hurt."

"Auntie, do you know that Cecil, one of the show's hosts, also told the Sheriff that Dad is the one that should be under scrutiny?"

"Yeah, I do, honey."

"You know I can't have that. Even though it might be a little dangerous for me, I need to help clear this matter up ASAP for both reasons. You know that."

"I know you want your kitchen back to normal. And you love your father and want to protect him. But trust me on this one, the police don't see him as a suspect."

"OK, thanks for sharing that."

"Now, I want to ask you something."

"Shoot."

"How did Zach get the powder?"

"I saw Denise, the sound girl that is sometimes special effects, give him the vial."

"Why?"

"Zach liked to pull pranks and he was going to fake foaming from the mouth and nose to play a prank on the crew. Denise helped him set it up."

"And how did it get into his respiratory passage

ways?"

"I saw him turn around. I think he snorted it."

"OK, that is similar to what is being reported by the TV crew members. Do you remember how long it took for the powder to choke him?"

"Not really. Time seemed to stop and it could have been a few minutes or more. Time just didn't seem to matter or register when it happened."

"That is not very helpful, but it is just like you, sweetie. Honest as can be."

"Aunt Mae, why are you asking me all this? The Sheriff already asked me most of those questions."

"I need to speak with someone I think I can trust to confirm some of the things the TV crew told me. And if you can't trust your family, who can you trust."

"No one!"

"Exactly. So thanks for the information and honesty."

"Well, I don't want to exaggerate or mislead you."

"I do have one more question. Did you see the vial before Denise gave it to Zach?"

"No. And that's the big question, isn't it? Who had access to the vial and put the slush powder in it?"

"Sure is. If we know the answer to that, we know

who is responsible and probably why this happened."

I paused, then decided to just ask what I was thinking. "Did you find anything on the vial, like a fingerprint or something?"

"I'm not supposed to tell you that. But no. And no DNA either. The state lab looked at the vial every which way. But remember, you don't know that!"

"Okay. I appreciate you sharing, thank you. So how are we going to find who filled the vial with slush powder?"

"I was hoping to talk to you about how to answer that, sweetie. That's why I'm really here, to be honest."

I stared blankly at her. My Aunt Mae, Deputy Owens, was actually asking for my help.

I rubbed my tired eyes. "I will do anything I can to help, you know that. But that question is above my pay grade."

"Maybe not. You have to promise to keep this under wraps and we never talked today. Understand?"

"Sure."

"The TV show gave us a copy of the video from when Zach died. They put a file online for the police to review. But like with the powder, you and your friends are pretty resourceful and I am hoping that if

I give you access to the video, you might find something. The state police say there is nothing there, but I need to know for sure that's the case. I am thinking Ida and Piper might take a look. They cannot tell anyone about it and must report directly to me what they find. Understood?"

"Yes."

"Give me a napkin to write down how to access the file."

I took a bar napkin and placed it on the bar in front of Aunt Mae. At that very moment, Lily and Edith came into the pub through the front door. Edith raised her voice while waving me over and said, "Ginger, you better come out here, there is something you need to see."

I smiled at Aunt Mae as a way of saying please give me a minute and went to the front door to see what Lily thought was so important. On stepping out onto the sidewalk, I could see there were protesters assembling and organizing. It seemed there were varying opinions as evidenced by the plethora of signs they carried. It appeared that some wanted to come visit The Grumpy Chicken and honor Zach. Then there were others that appeared to hate the pub, because they claimed it killed Zach.

I could not help but think about how Cecil had accused my father Tom of setting up his co-host. But how could the fans know of Cecil's accusation? I spotted Deputy Wise making an attempt to coral the protesters and keep them out of the street. But his attempts failed, and for now, Main Street was closed. I looked at Lily and Edith. "Well, this is first for Potter's Mill."

I made my way back into the pub and back to Aunt Mae at the bar. I sniffed and rubbed my nose. "I know this is going to sound strange. But you may want to give Deputy Wise a hand out front. Protesters are shutting down Main Street."

"What? I was out there ten minutes ago."

"I know. Not much like anything I have seen here, but go look for yourself."

Aunt Mae handed me the napkin with some writing now on it. "Take a look at the video and let me know what you find. And remember, no one is to know you took a look, or even that you know about this copy." She put her hat back on. "Now let's see what in the world is going on outside."

"Well at least we don't have to worry about people running the one stop light. No one can drive on Main Street with the number of protesters."

Mae looked at me and smiled. "The Sheriff never had an excuse to mount up and ride down protesters on Main Street. He always preferred a horse to his car and I bet he is here in ten minutes on a horse."

Dog replied from the end of the bar. "I'll take that bet."

I stared Dog down. "Dog, do you think betting with a police officer on duty is a good idea? And I think you forget I don't allow gambling in the pub."

Mae said, "It's okay sweetie. It will give me a chance to get my twenty dollars back from him I lost last week."

My jaw hung. "Auntie! I didn't hear that! I'm shocked."

Mae chuckled. "I've lived here longer than you, honey. I know people and what goes on inside the Chicken. It's fine. When you were a little girl, your father used to make more money taking bets than selling drinks."

Tom heard that and piped up. "Still know how to place a bet better than any man in town!"

I yelled back at him, "Yeah, but times change and we have to be more careful now. Just saying."

Mae gave me a hug and whispered. "See you soon! See what you can find in the video."

I replied in a low voice. "You seem pretty sure we'll find something even though the state police didn't find a thing."

"Just a hunch I have. You do have more at stake than them with your kitchen closed. And you're more resourceful. Don't let me down." Mae released me and patted my shoulder, then turned and left.

Chapter Eight

I took the napkin with the web site address and password to the office. I opened the door and entered to see Ida and Piper doing research. "I got something else for you to look at. But you have to promise not to mention anything about it. To anyone!"

Ida looked at me like my ex-husband used to when I told him to take the trash out. She finally said, "Well, no hellos but you have more work for us? Sounds like someone is getting too big for her britches."

I smiled at her. "You'll like this one even though it is more work. The show put a copy of the Zach choking video online so the police could inspect it. And Mae just gave me the information to access it."

Piper leaned back in her chair. "Wow. She asked us to take a look?"

"I know, but only the three of us can know about this. Got it?" I stared at both of them for a moment to wait till they nodded yes. "I was surprised she asked us to help, too, but not as much as I was to see protesters out front."

Ida sat up straight. "What? Protesters here in little ole Potter's Mill? That's something you don't see everyday."

Piper added, "Um. That's not something you see in Potter's Mill, like ever."

I waved my hand at the door. "Go take a look if you have to, but they are here. Out front and they've shut down Main Street. But after a quick look, I need you to take a real close gander at that video. Maybe you two can find something the police missed."

Ida went back to work. "I'd rather analyze the video. I tried to find a copy of it already. This makes things easier."

Piper rose. "I would like to see the protesters and get some photos for the paper. Maybe even interview a few. But I'll be back, Ida." And she left to go outside.

Ida typed in the information and opened the file. She started to play the video and noted, "The quality is good. But from what I am seeing, it shows pretty much what we saw with our own eyes that night."

"Play it again."

Ida restarted the video and we watched for a while. After a couple of minutes. I asked, "Can you stop it there? Go back a few seconds."

Ida scowled. "What? This is about the end of the video."

"I know. But I want to see something one more time. Go back, please."

Ida complied and restarted the video. I blurted out, "Stop! Right there."

Ida scratched her head. "So what are we looking at. Zach is already on the floor and Tyler just went to help him."

"Exactly. Look at Cecil. He is still trying to ignore the whole scene. Just for a couple of seconds right after Tyler sprinted to Zach, Cecil should have responded too. But he didn't."

"I think you've been getting too little sleep, Ginger. That is pretty thin."

"Yeah. But it still strikes me as odd. I was thinking Cecil wasn't our guy. But this is odd and increases his chances, in my mind at least, of being guilty."

Ida tilted her back and exhaled. "I have to admit it's a tad weird, but it doesn't prove a thing. It's not even significant."

"You're right. But there are two significant things I do see. One, even though he is out of the shot when he does it, it's pretty obvious Zach snorted that powder. And two, Zach was playing a prank. He displays all the signs of someone fooling around. And he loved himself far too much to consider killing himself."

"So?"

"So that means he didn't substitute something on his own to commit suicide and he sniffed the powder in the vial given to him by Denise. So either Denise put something other than seltzer and food color in the vial, or someone changed it."

Ida huffed. "That question again. It keeps coming up. But I have to agree it's the one question that needs to be answered."

"So how do we figure it out?"

Ida shrugged. "Start with Denise. You haven't spent a lot of time talking to her, but she gave the vial to Zach. I would think we should try to find out when she filled it. If it was left unattended, and for how long. Then that might give you an idea of who could of had the access to switch it."

I laughed. "Wow. Some decent answers and for once you didn't have to use a computer."

Ida was not as amused. "I have a brain too, you know."

"Yes, you do have a brain, but it is always occupied with a computer screen. But for once you put that bad boy to use the old fashioned way. Thanks for that! Now, have you or your electronic creepers found any dirt on Denise Anderson. Seems she is next on the list of things to do."

"Of course. She's a bit of a stereotype. Appears she spends tons of money on clothes even though her salary doesn't support it. She must have someone giving her money to buy her wardrobe."

"What? Why did you wait to tell me that?"

"Just found out. Her credit history revealed a lot. And I have to tell ya, I noticed she seems to be wearing some expensive jewelry. But I haven't found anything online to show she bought the shiny bobbles herself."

"You know, you're right. When she first talked to me, I saw an expensive tennis bracelet on her wrist."

"Wow! I didn't think a pub owner that sometimes displays tomboy tendencies, knew what a tennis bracelet was."

I blinked a couple of times, feeling like I had been slapped. "I don't have tomboy tendencies!"

"Not really, and I like the ribbons you have been using lately to tie your hair back. Very pretty and feminine. But you border on being tomboy when you're being bossy. And you should wear something other than generic brand jeans once in a while."

"I'm just focused and need to get my kitchen back. You're taking things too personal."

Ida laughed out loud. "Well, then everyone takes things too personal because I have heard just about everyone say you can be bossy."

"Ouch. I'll work on that. Thanks for telling me."

"It's alright. Someone has to lead us. And I know I give you a hard time, but you do a pretty good job."

I eyed her closely. "Do you need to borrow money? I've never heard you give a compliment before."

Ida sipped her coffee then smiled. "Don't get used to it. You may never hear one again."

"Well, thanks. But now I should go have a chat with Denise. I'm not sure if she'll talk to me, but only one way to find out." I turned to leave with new purpose.

Ida yelled and her words chased after me as I left. "Good luck."

***

It was about two thirty and I knew Denise would be back at the The Fluffy Pillow. Dottie, the B&B owner, met me when I entered and told me Denise was up in her room. Dottie called her from the front desk phone and then handed me the phone. Denise agreed to come down and meet me in the lobby. It took about ten minutes, but she finally appeared. She looked different. Her normally coiffed hair was held back with a blue head band, her face had no makeup, and she wore a white robe instead of designer jeans.

I started, "Thanks for meeting me with no notice. I hope this is not a bad time?"

"No. I was sleeping. We usually sleep during the day to be fresh for the night time shoots."

"Sorry. Didn't mean to wake you. But I did want to ask you a few questions."

Denise smiled. "Sure. I told you before to let me know if I could help with anything."

I saw she was wearing a ring with huge diamonds. "That's real generous of you. Thanks." Denise smiled in response, and after a short pause, I continued. "The vial of powder is of interest to everyone, as I'm sure you know."

Her smile disappeared. "Of course. It's all the police wanted to talk about the last couple of times I met with them."

"So, when did you fill it?"

Denise was now frowning. "Wow. You sound just like the police. Why do you care about any of this?"

"Because I need to reopen my kitchen and clear my father's name. And as a bonus, I also need to get rid of the protesters that are now keeping my customers away. I'm just trying to stay in business. And best way to do that is to figure out what happened to Zach."

She stared at me. "I never met anyone so focused and..." She paused a moment. "...and tough. Okay. Ask your questions."

"Thanks. So when did you fill the vial?"

"That morning, the day Zach died. I bought some seltzer tablets and food coloring at the pharmacy.

Then I crushed the tablets and filled the vial in my room. Left it there till that night, when we started shooting."

"Was your room locked?"

Denise shrugged. "Yes. Of course."

"Did anyone else have access to your room?"

"No. Not that I know of. I slept in the room for a good portion of the day, like usual."

"And when did you get up?"

"About five. To shower and clean-up, then get something to eat. Then I went over to the pub."

"Did you take the vial with you?"

"Yes. I had it my pocket."

"Was it in your pocket the whole time, till you gave it to Zach?"

"No. I took it out at the pub and put it on the table where I was working. You know, a lump in my Calvin's is unsightly so I had to empty my pockets to look good."

"Denise, this is real important. Where did you put the vial when you were at the pub?"

"On the table with my copy of the script. I put it in a paper bag so no one would see what it was."

"Did anyone move the bag, or open it?"

"No. I don't think so."

"Where was your table that night? Do you remember?"

"You were there and saw me. I always set up a place to work during a shoot, away from the action. I used a table in the corner of your dining room."

"I remember that. You've been a doll. This was very helpful. Thanks."

"I'm not sure why it's helpful. I've told the police all this."

"I know, but sometimes it helps to go over things one more time. Thanks again. See you tonight."

"Alright. Thanks again. See you later." She waved at me as I rose and left.

***

I headed back to the pub. I had too much to think about and was in my own little universe when walking back into the Chicken. But Dixie's voice shattered it all. "Ginger, these son's of a camera lens are wrecking everything!"

I looked around and saw technicians crawling all over one end of my bar. The end where the boys sat. Then I heard drilling and yelled, "Stop! What do you think you're doing?"

One of the technicians replied. "The big guy told us we could do whatever needed to monitor this area. To set the meters and hide the wires, I have to drill through this part of the bar."

"You can't drill my bar. Stop it now."

Dad appeared from the kitchen. "Ginger, it's okay. I told them it's alright. We need to document the chicken ghost and they are just setting up to do that."

Tyler was there directing the work. "EMF and sound meters have to be set. We're just drilling some small holes to keep everything out of sight and safe. We'll repair everything good as new before we leave. I promise."

"I hope the damage will be repaired better than new."

Tyler nodded. "Yes. Our craftsman are the best and you'll never know we were here."

"Thanks." But I wanted to say more, ask him questions. So sometimes you have to just trust your gut, and this was one of those times. I was not sure why, but I blurted out, "Say Tyler, can I have a word with you, in private?"

"I guess. But why?"

"I want to ask you some questions. And I'm not sure when we might be able to talk alone again."

He shrugged. "Okay, lead the way. I'm not sure there is a private place in here to be had to be alone, though."

"There isn't. Follow me and I'll buy you a cup of coffee too."

I led us out of the Chicken and we walked across the street, through the protesters, to the sandwich shop. The owner Velma Harris spotted us as we entered. She waved. "Ginger, haven't had you in here in a while. But Lord knows, you've been a busy girl lately. And those protesters have been a handful for sure. But glad to have ya."

"Good to see you, too, Velma. This is Tyler Fells, he's one..."

"I know who he is. The whole world knows the hosts of The Ghost Hounds. Hello and welcome to my sandwich shop Mr. Fells. So sorry about Zach."

"Thanks. And call me Tyler. And it's nice to meet you Velma."

I asked. "Velma, you have a fresh pot of coffee on?"

"No. But I will brew a new one just for you too."

"Thanks. Can we grab a booth?"

"Sure. Sit wherever you like."

I smiled at her in thanks, then I took the booth that gave us the best privacy. I didn't waste any time after we sat. "So, what do you think the blue blobs were the other night?"

Tyler leaned back. "To be honest, I think it was an

apparition. But I need more data to confirm it."

"Did you tell my father that?"

"No, of course not. I don't like making statements until I'm sure. You seem level headed so I don't mind discussing it with you. But I have yet to draw a conclusion."

"That's very nice of you. I appreciate you being open with me."

"Now can you tell me something. Why don't you believe in the ghost chicken? It's clear you don't. But all the stories I've heard and things I've seen in the short time here tell me something unusual is going on inside your pub."

I chuckled. "I've heard all the chicken ghost stories growing up and the Grumpy Chicken is a big part of my life. And I've seen and heard some strange things, yes. But there always seems to be another possible explanation. So like you, I just don't want to jump to false conclusions which could scare off customers."

Tyler smiled. "Seems we think alike."

Our coffee showed up and Velma bubbled at another chance to talk to Tyler. "I saw that one episode where you used that fancy equipment to document the spirit presence in that prison cell. It was so amazing."

Tyler smiled, but I could tell it was forced. "Thanks. A lot of people liked that episode."

Velma put the cream and sugar on the table and smiled. "Let me know if you need anything else." She then left, looking back over her shoulder one more time.

Tyler put some sugar in his coffee, but skipped the creamer. He continued, "Can you keep a secret?"

"There seems to be lots of secrets with your show. But sure."

"We staged that scene Velma just mentioned. Zach insisted on it. He was a spoiled little brat about things, but the producers and directors knew he had a nose for the dramatic. And it was good for ratings. Zach told me when we argued about staging the prison cell scene that it would make for one of the most remembered moments in the TV show's history. I hate to admit it, but he was right. More people mention that one shoot than any other."

"You clearly didn't like the showmanship aspect. But, you also sound like you miss Zach, maybe a little?"

"I do. We argued all the time, but that is what made it all work. Zach was all showmanship; I'm all science. Neither stands on its own with a show like this, so we provided balance to each other and made it work."

"So what are you going to do now?"

"I don't know. Cecil thinks he'll take Zach's place now. But that's not going to happen. Cecil doesn't have the talent."

"Or the looks!"

We both laughed and drank a little of our coffee. I asked, "Do you know Denise well?"

"Sure. We've worked together for a while now."

"You know she gave the vial of powder to Zach that killed him?"

"Yes. And that is why I have been thinking about it a lot."

"So have I. You have any thoughts on how a powder that could kill got into that vial?"

"Someone had to change it. Denise is a lot of things. But not a murderer. She has a kind heart and would never hurt a fly. Even a fly that she hates."

I played a little with my spoon. "I'm starting to understand that. But did you know she dated Zach for a while?"

"Sure. Everyone knew."

"She had access to the vial. And she was a former girlfriend. And she seems to wear clothes and jewelry beyond her means. Makes her a pretty strong suspect."

"Sure. It looks that way. But if you were going to frame someone to get suspicion away from you, wouldn't you make sure it looked like that person really did it? Denise is being framed to keep attention away from the real murderer. I'm sure of it."

I sipped my coffee and gazed at Tyler, studying his eyes. The eyes speak even when the lips are still. And what his eyes were telling me was that Denise did not do it.

Chapter Nine

After finishing my coffee with Tyler, I returned to the office to find Ida still working. I told her what I learned from Tyler and Denise.

Ida exhaled. "Well, it sounds like you think Tyler and Denise are no longer tier one suspects."

"I don't."

"So that leaves Scooter and Cecil as tier one suspects."

"Yep. But what about Kenny and Cory? They seem to have been lost in the shuffle."

"Oh! I didn't tell you? I don't think they knew Zach very well. I think you were right. The Sheriff talked to them that night, simply at random. They were just part of the crowd."

"How can you be so sure?"

Ida snorted. "Lily and Edith. They saw the Sheriff and just asked him. He told them that he was pretty sure they didn't do it."

"But that still leaves Stan the director?"

"Yeah, but Stan has not been the director all that long. Seems the show goes through a lot of directors and there is no motive I can find for Stan."

"So Scooter and Cecil it is."

I closed my eyes and thought. Then it hit me. "Ida, Denise said she put the vial in a paper bag. Do we know if it's still here?"

"What? How would I know that? What are you talking about and where was what?"

"On the table Denise was using. The paper bag she hid the vial in. It may be too late, but let's go see if it's still there."

"Why?"

"Aunt Mae."

Ida shrugged. "Okay. Be weird. I can handle it."

I left for the dining room and Ida followed. I made

my way to the spot I remembered seeing Denise working. And a paper bag with the pharmacy's logo was sitting on the floor in a dark corner near the table where Denise had been.

I said, "Ida, maybe the Grumpy Chicken was looking out for us. I can't believe we were this lucky. Can you get some tongs and a clean plastic bag from the kitchen."

Ida sighed and threw her hands in the air. "See, that's bossy."

"Just do it. Please?"

"Oh, since you said please, no problem me lady." She made a half curtsy and left to get the items.

I studied the floor and the table. I was hoping to also find a receipt. But I waited to do anything else as I didn't want to touch anything. Ida returned and I took the tongs. I used them to pick up the paper bag and looked inside. And I could see there was a receipt from the pharmacy. I tried to see what was listed on the receipt but couldn't see well enough. So I took the receipt out with the tongs and read the list of items; there was only two, seltzer tablets and food coloring. I placed the paper bag along with the receipt into the clean plastic bag with the tongs.

Ida said, "OK. I see we're playing TV detective. But why place a common paper bag into another bag."

"Aunt Mae said it the other day. The state labs can

look for DNA. Maybe the killer touched the paper bag or receipt when they swapped the powder and left us some DNA as a clue."

"You Nancy Drew'd me! Well aren't you full of surprises. So you going to give that to Mae?"

"Sure. I'm not sure how we all missed it. But we got a new piece of evidence now and the police should take a look at it."

Ida laughed. "You said it yourself. Maybe the grumpy chicken kept it hidden for you to find."

I glared at her. "I hope you're joking."

"Of course I am. I couldn't resist after setting up a webcam to look for its ghost. And it rials you up whenever someone blames the ghost fowl."

I chuckled a little. "There's the Ida I know." I looked at the plastic bag with its contents. It didn't matter how it happened. The fact was we now had a new, important piece of evidence.

I needed to bring the new find to Mae so the state labs could test it for DNA. I also knew she would want to know about what I saw in the video, so it was time to visit the police station and have a chat with my aunt.

I made the walk to the station and it took a little longer than usual. The protesters had grown in number and getting through the crowd gathered on Main Street was tedious.

I entered the police station and found Eunice on the phone, as usual. She waved at me and pointed towards Aunt Mae's desk. I waved in thanks and knew the way. I found her at her desk. She was hard at work but stopped when I appeared and leaned back in her chair. "Well, sweetie, so nice to see you. I'm almost afraid to ask, but what brings you down to the station?"

"Hello Auntie. I have two things for you. First I looked at the video and learned two things. One, Zach was playing around and thought he was playing a prank. Two, Zach snorted the powder in the vial. So he didn't use his own powder or commit suicide. So the question now is, who put the slush powder in the vial and when?"

"The state labs had a body language expert look at the video. He came to the same conclusion. Zach was fooling around. You have a pretty good eye for this."

"Well, to be honest, it was obvious. And Zach loved himself far too much to kill himself."

"Some of the crew told me the same thing, almost verbatim."

"Well, the other thing is this." I put the plastic bag with the paper bag and receipt inside on her desk.

Mae studied it a moment. "What's that?"

"The bag Denise hid the vial in just before the shoot. It could have DNA from someone if they touched the bag when they switched the powder."

Mae noted, "If someone switched it."

"Well, I don't think Denise did it. She likes her life on the show too much and enjoys the perks. Also, she doesn't seem like someone who would hurt another living thing. She seems to want to please people, not hurt them. So, I think it is more probable the powder was switched."

"There you go again. If it was switched."

"Yeah. But Denise said she bought seltzer tablets and food die at the pharmacy. The receipt here confirms what she said."

"We were hoping to find that receipt. Where did you find it?"

"In the corner of the dining room."

Mae went white. "How in the world did we miss that?"

"I'm not sure it was easy to see. Plus, the dining room is dark and everyone has been focused on the vial and the kitchen area. The paper bag she used to hide it before the prank was not really on the radar."

"We were looking for a receipt, not a paper bag. How did you find out she hid it in a bag."

"I just asked her."

Mae smiled. "So did we. But she seems to have been more open with you. Denise told me she put the vial under her script, or something. I guess the something was the paper bag."

"I guess. I need to ask you one more thing. If Denise did put seltzer and food coloring in the vial like she said, shouldn't there have been some residue? Did the lab find any seltzer residue in the vial?"

Mae stared at me then answered. "You can be too smart for your own good!" She took a deep breath, then laughed. "Yes, they did. I was afraid that was what you were going to tell me. Why you thought Denise switched the powder. But that would also mean you broke into the lab's computers, which is a crime by the way. I'm relieved you came to that conclusion on your own and not by hacking the state police. That Ida is going to get herself, and maybe you into trouble one day. Be careful with her, sweetie." She touched my cheek to let me know she worries about me. "But seems this all indicates the powder was switched and the bag could be an important clue. Good work Ginger. Thanks for bringing it to me."

"You're welcome. But you know, it's what we do in a small town like Potter's Mill."

"Yes it is." She smiled and picked up the plastic bag, studying its contents. "Did you touch this?"

"Nope. Used clean tongs. And I isolated the area around the table and corner where I found it so you can take another look."

"I'll get someone from the state labs to come over to scour the area. And I need you to fill out a statement and chain of custody for this piece of evidence. I don't like you getting involved in police business. I want you to know I'm cutting you some slack because I know you need your kitchen back."

"And the protesters gone. No one wants to fight through the crowd to come in and have a beer. And I certainly don't like having my father or the pub blamed or associated with Zach's death."

Mae looked at the ceiling for a few seconds. "You know, the protesters have been bothering me. Why are they protesting? Why do they blame the pub?"

"I was wondering the same thing. It's odd."

"Well, from what I see, only one person made accusations against the pub. Or more specifically, Tom."

I exhaled. "I know. Cecil. He keeps coming up on my radar. And did I mention, his reaction right after Zach died was strange. Now he thinks he is the new Zach for the show. You know, he might not be as clumsy as I thought."

Chapter Ten

The Ghost Hounds crew returned at eleven o'clock that night and started prepping for a shoot in the dining room. I saw Cecil and went to have a word with him. But he saw me coming and held his hand up like a traffic cop signaling a stop. "I hear you're going around asking lots of questions of lots of people. I have no interest in answering any more questions. The police have asked every possible question and it's time to move on."

"I'm not trying to pester you or be an annoyance. I just wanted to talk to you. I need to get my kitchen open again and I was hoping you might help me do it."

Cecil eyed me, doubt in his dull green eyes. "You make me nervous. I don't know why, but you do."

"What have I done to make you nervous?"

"You're his daughter for starters. Your father is the one who made us come out here. And if we didn't come here Zach would still be alive."

"How do you know that?"

"You heard him. Zach said it just before he died. The chicken that haunts this place choked him. If we didn't come here the spirit wouldn't have killed him."

"I'm not sure a ghost can kill. If there was a ghost. I lived here all my life and have never seen a spirit in here."

"But the stories everyone tells?"

"Some jars breaking in the night? Some odd sounds every now and then? Not that unusual in an old building."

"This place is haunted. I know it. And your chicken killed Zach. He said so himself just before he died and it is on tape."

"I was told he plays pranks all the time. How do you know it wasn't a prank?"

Cecil paused. "I know it was the chicken."

I looked at him sideways. "I know you have work to do, so I'll leave you to it. Thanks for taking a couple of minutes to talk."

Cecil didn't speak. He just weakly waved his hand and turned to leave. The meeting with Cecil was odd, just like everything else about him. I wasn't sure what to do with myself next, but I saw the gang had assembled around Lily and Edith's table to watch the next shoot. So I went to join them.

On the way over, I ran into Dad. "What are you doing talking to that bollix."

"Just thought I would ask him a few questions. But you're right, Dad. He's stubborn and unpleasant."

"That's the nicest thing I could say about him." Dad smiled as he went over to help Dixie bring a tray of drinks.

I resumed my way over to be with the gang. As I was selecting a seat, Guardrail spoke as he looked at his old spot back at the bar. "I'm not sitting there, ever again."

Lily replied, "You don't have to lie to us, dear. It's okay if you want to sit here with us." I sat with Piper and Ida at the adjacent table. Lily leaned over to whisper to Piper, "He's not scared of the chicken spirit. I think he's sweet on us now." I think I saw Piper shudder in response.

Dixie came over with the drinks and took a seat with us. "I can't make a living with those protesters. No one in here drinking means no tips." I looked at Dixie, intending to say something supportive but she assumed otherwise. "I'm sorry, Ginger. I wasn't being selfish. I know this is hard for you too."

"No Dixie. It's okay. This is hurting both of us. There's no doubt about that. But I have an idea to throw a sort of concert Friday night when Star plays. Maybe we can have some drink specials to help draw more people, too. At least we can still sell drinks if people are willing to come inside."

Dixie nodded. "That sounds good. But we need to get rid of the protesters. How do we do that?"

I sighed. "Simple answer, solve the crime."

Dog jumped in. "Don't you mean potential crime?"

"No, I am pretty sure this is a crime now. Zach snorted the powder from the vial and he clearly thought he was playing a prank. The video confirmed that. He didn't think it would hurt him so it wasn't suicide. That means someone put a lethal powder in that vial. And that *is* a crime."

Bones had been quiet for the last couple of days, but chose this time to pipe up. "I wondered about that, boss. Maybe it was just an accident and Denise *thought* she put seltzer in the vial?"

"Good point, Bones. Glad you're paying attention. Living single has freed your brain to focus on other things."

Dad had come back with Dixie and was sitting next to Bones. He smacked the teenager on the back of the head. Either Dad was jealous of Bones love life, or he was trying to knock some sense into the young man. Bones rubbed the back of his head as he gently poked Dad in the arm to respond. It warmed my heart to see Bones knew that my father had taken him under his wing, almost like a son.

Bones repeated. "So how do you know it wasn't an accident?"

I answered. "The receipt. It backs up Denise's story. And the state labs found seltzer residue in the vial. Again, consistent with Denise's story"

Digger threw his hands in the air. "So! You still need this solved quick. How do you do that?"

I raised my eyebrows. "We need that one piece of indisputable evidence. Simple as that. But I don't know if it even exists. And if it does, how do we find it?"

Piper leaned back in her chair. "Some questions are so easy to ask, but impossible to answer."

Ida was drinking something with an umbrella in it. I didn't even know we had any of those frilly things left to garnish our drinks with. She said, "The best thing to prove something today is with video. Cameras are everywhere today and more and more people get caught doing illegal stuff on camera."

Dog replied, "Too bad we don't have cameras all over the pub like they do in London. We might have recorded the ole switcheroo with the powder and who did it."

Ida popped up and leaned on the table. "Dog, I can't believe I am going to say this, but you're a genius. Why didn't I think of this before. We have one camera recording events in here. The pickled egg jar camera. I haven't looked at it for a couple days."

I gasped, "Can we be that lucky?"

Edith prompted, "Well, what are we waiting for."

The gang abandoned the TV shoot in the dining room and headed to the office to view the pickled egg jar video with Ida. After cramming the entire gang into my office, Ida set up her laptop with the largest screen so we could all see it. Then she played the webcam video from the night of Zach's death.

Lily asked, "Why are things fluttering?"

Ida answered, "I have it on fast forward so we can watch the whole day's video more quickly. Sometimes it just flickers when played with fast forward."

After about five minutes, the jar seemed to move. Just a little. Ida pounced on the keyboard. "That was more than just flickering of the video." She stopped the video and backed it up. Then she replayed it slower and we all saw the jar moved slightly to one side and spun just a little.

I asked, "What could make a large jar move like that?"

Dog answered, "A blue blob chicken ghost!"

No one else spoke. Ida replayed it and there was no doubt. The jar moved on its own. We scanned the rest of that day's video, but found nothing else.

Ida finally spoke. "I'll scan the rest of the other day videos. But it appears the webcam didn't catch anyone messing with the vial. Not surprising, the camera was pointed at the bar, not the table where Denise was working."

I muttered, "So that was a bust. I knew we weren't that lucky."

Guardrail put his arm around me. "It was a long shot. We'll find another way to figure this out. We're the Grumpy Gumshoes!"

Piper crumbled a piece of paper and threw it at the big guy. "That's not helping! No one likes that name."

I said, "He's right. We checked the jar video and it was a long shot. But nothing is there so now it's time to move on. What do we do next?"

Ida jumped in. "Well, we have one suspect left – Cecil. I think we need to find everything there is to know about him. If he did it, there must be some clues we can find."

I added, "We haven't really looked hard at Scooter yet. Maybe it's time."

Ida replied, "He has arms bigger than Guardrail. That's not a man to get upset. You better be careful if you plan on talking to him. I'm not sure he did it either. He's a real nice guy and I have found nothing after his divorce was finalized that makes him a suspect."

I thought for a few seconds. "I think we need to do our due diligence and check him out to make sure we can focus on Cecil. And I'm not sure I'm the right person to talk to him. If Guardrail were to talk to him and see what he could learn, we would have a chance to sneak into his room over at The Fluffy Pillow. Maybe we can find some of the slush powder left in his room, or something like that."

Guardrail pouted. "I never interrogated someone. How do you expect me to do it?"

Ida objected, "Is this really necessary?"

I shrugged, "Yeah. Scooter has a potential motive and we haven't ruled him out. So, Guardrail, just talk to him. Ask him some questions about the incident. See if he knows anything about slush powder and the vial. He might tell you something that shows he knew Denise had the vial or that a prank was set up."

Guardrail shook his head. "I don't know. This sounds wrong. Can I take Dog?"

I nodded. "If you think it will help."

Dog waved his hand in the air. "No way. Don't drag me into this."

Ida jumped in. "So if the boys talk to Scooter, who is going to sneak into his room? This is crazy and not needed."

I looked at Ida a little confused. Then I turned to Piper. "It should be just the two of us."

Piper laughed out loud. "Oh no! I went on a stake out with you once and it did not go well. No way."

I replied. "It worked alright in the end. And this will too. I need my kitchen open and those protesters gone."

Piper stopped laughing. "If we get caught, I'm

telling the police it was all your idea."

I held my hand out to shake. "Deal. So when do we do this?"

Edith piped up. "I know Scooter goes to the waffle place in the morning. After they finish shooting."

Lily added, "Seems he likes that new waitress more than the food. All the boys seem to like her."

Ida interrupted, "Scooter told me he likes the waffles."

Edith continued, "Whatever the reason, you can find him there in the morning."

I sighed. "So. Tomorrow morning. Guardrail, you need to keep him there for at least a half hour to give us time."

Guardrail shook his head. "I don't like this. It's not what I'm good at."

Ida wrinkled her nose. "I can't believe you're going to do this. It's too dangerous for someone I think is innocent!"

Piper ignored Ida and went into journalist mode. "So seven a.m."

I repeated, "Seven a.m." Guardrail reluctantly nodded in agreement.

***

I woke at six in the morning to get ready. I called

Dottie to confirm the arrangements. She liked having The Fluffy Pillow full and was not keen on getting rid of The Ghost Hound show. However, she knew we had to find the murderer. Eventually she agreed to leave Scooter's door unlocked after an early cleaning and gave me his room number. After that, she asked to be kept ignorant to anything involving our stake out and investigation.

So it was on and I met Piper in front of The Fluffy Pillow at seven. My heart was pounding and I struggled to think straight. I knew Piper was nervous too because she kept touching her long brown hair, which she had braided into a pony tail that flowed over one shoulder.

We made our way into the B&B and found Dottie at the counter. She halfheartedly waved at us and pointed to show the way to Scooter's room.

We found the door easily, and as expected, it was unlocked and we went in. Once inside, Piper said, "Well that was better than our last attempt at illegal entry. At least we got in the door this time."

"Don't be so negative, Piper. And get looking for something we can use. We don't have much time."

We checked the dresser, bathroom, nightstands, all the obvious places. The room was not that large and after a few minutes, Piper gasped and held up a lacy black bra. "The big muscles always lure the girls in. Seems Scooter has been enjoying his stay in Potter's Mill."

I didn't know what to say. "You jealous?"

"Don't be silly. He's not my type." She threw the undergarment back on the floor.

"I'm not sure why we're acting like we're back in high school. Maybe it's the nerves from breaking into someone's room. But he's exactly your type."

Piper scowled at me. "Miss know it all. He's too old for me. So what is my type..." Suddenly the window shattered with glass flying everywhere and a rock tumbled to a stop on the floor.

I sprinted to the broken window to see Dog Breath outside waving furiously, combined with sporadic pointing towards the front door of the B&B. I turned to Piper. "We need to get out of here. Now! Someone is coming."

"Crimony on a biscuit! Just once, can't we stay quiet!" Piper ran to the door as she spoke. I followed and we made a hasty exit, using the back door of The Fluffy Pillow to leave.

Chapter Eleven

Piper and I ran back to the pub and for once found my office was empty. I sat at my desk to catch my breath and scanned the two laptop screens in front of me. I felt so stupid for not knowing what I was looking at.

Piper's breathing returned to normal. "So that was a bust!"

"I didn't find anything. You?"

Piper chuckled. "Yeah. You saw what I found. And I learned someone is buying better underwear than me."

I scowled at Piper. "That's not helpful. We risked a lot and learned nothing."

The door to my office opened and Guardrail and Dog Breath entered. I asked, "How did you get into the pub?"

"You're not supposed to know, but Dixie gave me a key a while ago. Don't ask why, but we were looking out for you. Trust me."

"I'm going to need to talk to you more about why you have a key to my business and home later. But for now, can you please tell me why Dog had to bust a window at The Fluffy Pillow?"

Guardrail sighed, then stood straight. "It didn't go

well with Scooter. He seems to like his privacy at the end of his work day. He decided to leave almost immediately after I started talking to him."

"So Dog just decided to throw a rock through the window of the room we were in?"

"Well, yeah. When I saw Scooter was leaving, I spilled my coffee on him and Dog took off to warn you. Of course he was supposed to use a pebble to catch your attention, not a boulder to break the window."

Piper broke into laughter. "Let me get this straight. You didn't talk but spilled hot coffee on him to slow him down? And then Dog ran out so he could head over to warn us?"

"Yeah. It worked. It took two or three minutes to get him cleaned up. The new waitress helped. Seems she liked helping him and he likes talking to her more than me."

I asked, "So Dog, how did you know what room we were in?"

"I could see the lights were on in only a couple of rooms, so I threw rocks at both of them. But the window in your room broke."

Piper laughed again. "Dog, why didn't you just come inside and ask Dot to help you?"

Dog shrugged, "I admit, yours was a better plan, but I didn't think of it."

Piper continued. "Well, I know one thing for sure. We stink at stake outs."

Guardrail hung his head. "I know. But I told you I didn't think I could handle an interrogation. Did you find anything?"

I said, "No, we didn't have much time. But everything in his room did seem normal."

Piper chuckled. "Normal is a relative term. So what do we do now?"

I looked again at the computer screens. "I want to talk to Ida. Cecil is the only one to accuse the chicken for Zach's death. I am thinking he is responsible for the protesters. And everything about him is odd. I think we should have looked in his room instead."

Piper scoffed. "We should have thought of that last night."

I nodded. "I know. But we didn't."

Piper's phone rang and she answered. "Ida! You're ready? I'll meet you out front of the Chicken, let you in." Piper left to retrieve her.

They returned a few minutes later, and on entering the office, Ida glared at me sitting behind the desk. "I thought the hack shack was still in business."

I said, "It is, but this is still my office."

Ida pinched her lips. "Fair enough. But I need to

ask you to move if you want me to work."

I answered, "Fair enough, me lady!"

Ida chuckled. "Ouch, you didn't like that one yesterday?"

I replied, "No, I did not."

The rest of the group looked at the two of us confused. So I offered, "Long story, but let's just say I know I can be domineering. But I don't like being called bossy. So I'm working on it."

Dog shrugged. "You _are_ the boss. So it goes with the territory."

Guardrail jumped in. "No one is the boss! We're all equal. But you know, Ginger, you can be a little alpha female."

I turned to Guardrail. "You're right. We're all equals. Can we drop this and get back to what to do next?"

Dog Breath piped up. "Get breakfast. I'm hungry."

We all looked at him and Piper spoke. "You know what, I'm hungry too. Guess breaking windows and illegal entry makes a person hungry."

Dog mumbled, "I didn't mean to break it."

Guardrail said, "Won't it look odd if I go back to the waffle place so soon?"

I replied, "Guardrail, what has been normal since

that TV crew showed up in town? I think it will be fine." And with that, we left to get a hot breakfast at Johnnie Gilbert's waffle place.

I realized the warm breakfast was the first time in days I sat and ate a proper meal. And the company of Dog Breath, Guardrail, Piper, and Ida made me feel better. I had serious money problems with losing a couple of days worth of sales, but they made me laugh and feel more optimistic.

We were done and enjoying one last cup of coffee when Piper asked, "So, you going to pay Dot for the broken window?"

I replied, "Sure, when I have some cash coming in again. It's the least I can do. Wait a minute, Dog broke the window. Dog you should pay."

Dog shook his head no. "Why? I did my job and warned you."

Piper added, "Because you broke it and you didn't have to."

I intervened, "I'll talk to Dottie, let her know we'll pay for it. I think we should all chip in." The group nodded in agreement.

That is when we heard it. The police siren was wailing at full volume and it appeared to head away from the Main Street strip.

I noted, "For a small town, there is a lot happening this week."

Ida added, "That's for sure...can't remember ever seeing this much happening in Potter's Mill. And I told you Scooter is not our man and that you would find nothing. So, I need to go back and check more on Cecil. See if we can confirm he arranged the protests."

I added, "I need to go, too. Talk with Dottie."

Piper asked, "So should we all plan on meeting at the Chicken later today?"

I replied, "Yeah, lets say four o'clock. Gives us enough time to take care of personal business but it's early enough to avoid the happy hour crowd in the pub." I snickered. "Well it used to be a crowd."

I left the waffle place and headed over to The Fluffy Pillow. I talked with Dottie about the broken window and she was upset. But she eventually understood and thanked us for offering to pay for it. When I was almost done, Kenny the boom operator came over and said, "Scooter is a good guy. What were you doing in his room?" I stared at him in disbelief and he could see it. So he continued, "I like the laid back breakfast here and was reading my book in peace and quiet over there." He pointed to an arm chair nearby. "It was hard not to hear."

I must have blushed. "I'm sorry. I need my business back and the only way to make that happen is to find out what happened to Zach."

"Well, I'm sure this is hard on you. But sneaking into someone's room is illegal. You shouldn't have done that."

"I know. I'm sorry. We won't do it again."

He grinned. "I'm not sure you need to apologize to me. And Scooter was the wrong guy. Cecil is the one acting odd. But you didn't hear it from me."

I looked at him a moment and tilted my head to one side. "Thanks. I think I understand."

He chuckled. "Good. Then you know we didn't talk this morning, right?"

"I talked to Dottie. No one else." I winked to confirm I knew he was trying to help.

Kenny left and Dottie whispered, "What am I supposed to do now?"

I replied, "Simple. Fix your window. The one a protester broke in anger. And you never saw or talked to Kenny this morning."

She giggled a little. "I get it! It's always so quiet and boring in here. I thought it was exhilarating when The Ghost Hounds booked here. But things just keep getting more interesting."

"Well, please use your discretion for now. We still have no idea who we can trust. I need your help to get this solved and my business back. Tell no one."

"I understand. You can count on me." Dottie was talking faster than usual, in a whisper. "And you didn't hear this from me." She winked, imitating how I had with Kenny. "Cecil just left a while ago, acting odd. Then I heard the police siren. It may be connected."

I chuckled at this version of Dottie. "Thanks. I appreciate it. See ya soon. Come over to the Chicken and have drink with us if you can get away for few minutes."

Dottie winked again. "I might just do that. See ya later."

Chapter Twelve

It had been three days since Zach's death and time seemed to be uncontrollably slipping away. Now three thirty in the afternoon, I expected some of my friends to start showing up to regroup at four o'clock as we agreed earlier in the day. I was partially right, Aunt Mae came through the front door unexpectedly.

I waved. "Well glad you came by. What's the special occasion that we get a visit from Potter's Mill's finest?"

Aunt Mae smiled. "Well I'm just your aunt. I'm not sure about all that finest business, but I wanted to talk to my favorite niece."

"That joke is getting old and I'm your only niece."

"So there's no competition and I'm not exaggerating."

"Thanks, then, I think. But what can I do for ya?"

She tilted her head toward a corner in the dining room, a secluded one. I went with her and we both took a seat, well out of earshot.

She said, "You aren't going to believe this, but that Cecil character left town this morning on foot. Set off an alarm on our computers we never heard or seen before. Scared the living daylights out of us."

"His ankle bracelet!"

"Bingo. And when we picked him up, he was acting real weird. So I took him to the station to question him and I noticed white powder on his fingers."

"Oh? Like slush powder?"

"I thought the same thing. So I took some swab samples and sent them to the state lab."

"Well now we have a couple of irons in the state lab fire. Did you hold him?"

"No. The Sheriff decided to let him out. Said we don't have enough to charge him, so he decided to let him have a second chance. But he's on a short leash now. I think the fact the bracelet worked so well helped the Sheriff make the decision to set him free."

"Well, I had dwindled the prime suspect list to Scooter and Cecil. But now I realize that was too superficial. I couldn't imagine the clumsy, chubby Cecil as a murderer. Scooter seems real nice, but he is more of a man's man. You know? So I was focused on him."

"I do know, sweetie. Scooter clearly likes lifting weights and takes care of himself. But looks aren't always a good indicator of what is going on inside a person. I've made the same mistake myself, so don't beat yourself up too bad."

"But now we just wait? Find out what the state labs come back with?"

"Pretty much, honey. But that's why I'm here. I know you've been working hard to reopen your kitchen. And that means Ida has been helping. Did she find anything else on Cecil?"

"No. But she is doing her thing, still, with those disturbing little electronic crawlers she sets up on the internet. Seems these Hollywood types are pretty good at keeping secrets, though."

"Can you let me know if she finds anything? I don't want this guy running out on us. So if you can give us a reason to charge him, we can hold him."

I actually felt a tear come to my eye. "Auntie, you have always treated me like a little girl. This is the first time you've reached out to me as an adult. I'm touched."

"That's so sweet. But don't get all gushy on me. We're trying to catch a murderer. That means you need to be tough."

"Funny, Denise told me I was tough. So guess I am up to the task in her eyes."

Aunt Mae laughed. "I've always used the word persistent to describe you. I guess you need to be a little tough to be persistent."

I chuckled. "I have to be tough. My dad brings a TV show home with him like it's normal! And now my cash flow is severely compromised."

"Oh don't be so hard on him. He has such a soft spot for you. You know he will always see you as his little girl. That is just the way it is with Dad's like him."

"I know." I fiddled my fingers, "But we have some real adult problems right now and it's all on me to fix them."

"I'm helping sweetie. I'll always be here for you." Mae flashed an understanding smile at me.

"Us too!" Guardrail, Dog Breath, and Digger had invaded out privacy.

I turned to them. "No one in this place understands discretion. We're having a private conversation."

Dog replied, "Seemed like you were discussing the case. We're part of the team."

Mae said, "Well, officially, we can't have civilians running around looking into police matters. But right now, seems we have a pretty good idea of the who done it, but no evidence to charge him. So we need to find that evidence."

Guardrail replied, "We were discussing that last night. It's why Piper and Ginger..."

I cut him off. "We came to the same conclusion and doubled up our efforts to find that evidence. Indisputable evidence we called it."

Mae replied. "Well that doubling of effort didn't by chance involve breaking a window in Scooter's room at The Fluffy Pillow, did it?" Silence ensued so she continued. "Ginger, the last thing I wanted to talk to you about is I cannot tolerate flaunting the laws, like let's say breaking and entering."

Dog added, "Technically, the breaking happened *after* the entering."

Mae smiled at me lovingly. "I'm trusting you a lot here to help us. But please don't put me or the Sheriff in a bad spot."

I nodded. "Understood. I know I can get a little too intense when I'm focused on something."

Mae sat back, laughed, and eyed the boys. "I was pretty sure Ginger was in the room. But I wondered which one of you threw the rock. Thanks for telling me Dog."

Dog's eyes became the size of our now infamous pickled eggs. "Am I in trouble?"

Mae laughed. "No. Dot told me you were going to fix it. That's good enough for me. But stay out of people's rooms!" She rose and gave me a little hug before she left. "See y'all around."

After Mae was gone, Dog spoke. "Whew! I thought I was going to jail."

Digger snapped back. "They don't put people in jail for breaking windows."

I asked, "So, now what? We have two items being tested by the state labs. And we are pretty sure it's Cecil. So how do we prove it?"

I explained the white powder Aunt Mae found on Cecil's fingers this morning. And the DNA test being done on the paper bag and receipt. Either one of those might be enough if they returned the right results. But we couldn't count on that. Ida had worked in the hack shack all day, it was time to pay her another visit. "Excuse me, I need to go talk with Ida."

Digger replied, "We're going with you. You know. The team thing."

I shrugged my shoulders. "Sure. Right now we need all the help we can get."

Ida was typing away when we entered and she stopped when she spotted us. "Is it four o'clock already?"

I answered her. "Almost. But we were wondering what you've found. You've been at it for a while now."

Ida grinned like a squirrel finding a bird feeder for the first time. "You came at a good time, I just made a breakthrough."

"So spill it!" I disliked when she tried to build up suspense to tell us she just read a few of someone's emails.

"Seems Cecil set up an alias. And he did a good job. It was hard to find, but I cracked it. Now I am reading emails he sent using that alias, and get this, not only did he arrange the protests, he paid for them."

I shrugged. "So, we suspected that he arranged it all."

Ida continued, "Cecil thought if there was controversy over Zach's death, it would catapult the show's ratings. And that he would become the new star to replace Zach."

I folded my arms. "Again, we kind of guessed that, but it is good to confirm it. However, that is not enough for the police to charge him. Anything about him buying slush powder or asking about it?"

"No. But I have a hundreds of emails still to get through."

Dog spoke up. "Can we help you?"

Ida laughed and leaned back in my chair. "No, I don't think I want anyone else using my good laptops. I can handle it."

I sighed. "So more waiting. I hate this."

Guardrail smacked the desktop and it made Ida jump. "I hate it too. What can we do?"

I took a deep breath and just said it. "We could try and sneak into Cecil's room when they come back to shoot tonight."

Digger rebutted. "No, Mae was clear and she is right. After the broken window, that's too risky now."

I tried a new direction. "When do they plan on coming back to shoot?"

Guardrail answered, "I think they're starting early, at seven tonight, since the place has been pretty empty."

"That will give Ida a few hours to get through the rest of the email. And it will give us a few hours to think about what we can do before Cecil comes back to the pub tonight." I was thinking out loud more than suggesting. Then it dawned on me. "Where is Piper?"

Ida answered, "She is at the Potter's Mill Oracle. Writing a story on the protesters."

"Great. I'll be back in about a half hour. In the mean time, boys can you do something for me?"

Dog was first to answer. "We always do what we can, you know that."

"I have a wacky idea. What if we can get Cecil to admit to something and get it on film, or whatever they call it now that it is digital."

Ida laughed. "We didn't get something on video by chance, so you now want to try and capture it on purpose. That's actually pretty smart."

"Yeah. If I get Piper in journalist mode, maybe she and I can get him to say something incriminating."

Digger asked, "But how do you get it on tape."

"That is what I need you to do. Can you find a camcorder or something to record with and get ready to film. I can tell Cecil we are doing our own small town version of behind the scenes and interview him with Piper. Maybe he can't handle the truth!" Everyone looked at me as if I spoke in tongues. "Oh for goodness sake. I thought everyone saw that movie."

Ida raised her eyebrows. "I'm not sure about your movie reference, but I can get a camera. A good one too."

I spun to look at her. "How?"

Ida blushed, "Well, I guess I should have told you. I've been seeing Scooter."

The collective gasp was loud. I tried to calm myself down, but my voice came out on the loud side. "How could you do that? He's a stranger and was a murder suspect!" And I guess you own black lacy bras too. Ugh...

She waved her hands randomly, like she was swatting away the issue. "I know. But only for a little while. And then it was clear he didn't do it. And when you get to know him, he's a sweet man."

Digger mumbled, "Sweet, as in big muscles sweet?"

I chided her. "I can't believe this. You could have been hurt. We need to talk, later. But for now, get the camera lined up and find whatever you can from those files you've discovered."

Ida looked at Guardrail, "You think you boys can operate a camera?"

He replied. "I guess, maybe Scooter can help show us how."

Digger added, "The three of us can handle it. But it has to be a mobile camera. Something we can move around with."

Ida nodded, "That's a good point. Let me call him and see what he can do."

Chapter Thirteen

Seven o'clock was approaching fast and I sat at the bar waiting for Piper to come back from her office. She wanted to retrieve her little voice recorder. Why, I could not tell you since we were already recording video, which included audio, but it made her more comfortable to have it. I was watching the boys play with the shoulder mounted camera in the dining room. Guardrail was chosen to operate the mobile camera. They could move around with the unit, but it was larger than expected and heavy.

Digger said, "The unit has to have power and it comes from this line." Digger pointed at a thick black cord. "Dog and me will move the power cable and help direct you, to make sure you don't trip. And remember, we need to keep Cecil on camera as long as Piper and Ginger are talking to him. So all three of us need to stay focused on moving with them."

I turned to Dixie, "Well, what could go wrong with this?"

Dixie laughed, "Let's just say they don't need to worry about making space on their mantle for an Oscar."

I joined her in laughter, "Maybe they do. Do they give out a comedy award?"

Dixie giggled. "Maybe."

Ida came rushing out through the swinging door from the kitchen into the dining room. She spotted me talking to Dixie and rushed over. "Come have a look at this, you'll want to see it."

I followed and realized Dixie was right on my tail. We set ourselves down in the office and Ida started a video on her computer. I recognized it. "Ida, we saw this. Why are you showing the jar video to us again?"

Ida waved at me. "Hush. Keep watching."

So I did. Ida had clearly worked with the video where the pickled egg jar moves. It was now enlarged and I could see scan lines moving down the screen. I asked, "What are those white bands rolling down over the image?"

Ida spoke faster than usual. "I enlarged and enhanced the footage of the jar moving. Let it finish and watch."

So again, I complied. And in a minute or so, I saw it. A reflection in one facet of the jar. It was a man and he picked up what looked like a bag on a table. It was not very clear and we could not see his face, but only one man was shaped like that and Dixie let loose. "Are you kidding me? That pear shaped weasel. He messed with the bag. But how did he know the prank had been set up?"

I was dumbfounded and mute. Then I found my voice. "I don't know Dixie. Ida, why did you go back to this video?"

She replied, "I'm not sure. I finished going through all the Cecil files and just thought about looking at it again."

I took a deep breath. "Well, I'm glad you did. This is pretty good and it all points at Cecil. But I'm not sure this is enough to arrest him."

"I agree, but it's clearly a man shaped like Cecil messing with a bag at the table where Denise was working." Ida beamed as she talked. "And get this! I almost missed it because of how it was labeled. But Cecil ordered a magician's kit. One that contained a powder used to perform a disappearing water trick. Slush powder."

I felt the air leave my body. "Well that is more like it. Why do you always bury your lead. Ida! I should call Aunt..." And then my phone rang.

In small towns, we talk to each other, face to face. The phone is not used near as much as in the city. So when my cell phone rang, it was usually an emergency. As I answered I saw it was Aunt Mae. "Hello, Aunt Mae? I was just going to call you. What can I do for ya?"

Mae talked slow and deliberate. "Sweetie, listen closely. The results came back on that paper bag. Cecil's DNA is on it. We need to bring him in. Is he there now?"

"No, I don't think so."

"Well our little tracker on his ankle says he just

walked there from the B&B. Keep him there and don't let him know anything is up. Okay? If he senses something is up, you stay clear of him."

"Will do. I can't believe this! You should be here in a couple minutes, right? So we don't have to do anything but stall him?"

"I'm waiting for the Sheriff to meet me here at the station, then we'll head over together. So I am guessing no longer than five minutes. Just talk with him, keep him there."

"See ya in a few then." The phone clicked off and as I expected, everyone was staring at me. "Slight change of plans." I rose to head back to the dining room, but stopped. "It might be best if y'all wait here. I'll be right back."

I headed out to the dining room, leaving Ida and Dixie in the office. As I came through the swinging door into the dining room, I saw Piper had returned. She was seated at the bar chatting with the boys working the camera. And Cecil was sitting next to her. Guardrail pointed at the camera and I got the message, it was running. The plan was to agitate Cecil enough to open up and we were set to go, but things had changed with Aunt Mae's call. So I made a snap decision, shoot the video as planned. An admission would only help with all the other evidence and it was as good a way to stall Cecil as any. "Piper, glad you're here. Cecil, did they explain that we thought it would be fun to set up a shoot of our own. A kind of Potter's Mills version of behind the scenes of The Ghost Hounds."

Piper smiled at Cecil. "Sounds like fun, right?."

I nodded. "Yeah. And Piper and I are the local hosts. Cecil, you can be our first interview, since you're already here."

Piper asked, "Do I look alright for TV?"

I put my hands on my hips. "Oh please! Don't worry about it. Look at me. I'm in my jeans as usual and no makeup. You look great."

Cecil was not amused. "I never agreed to an interview. You're assuming a lot."

I replied to him. "Well, you're early and maybe we can have a drink and just talk a little. It will be good for your image and your show. You know, show the world how down to earth you are. And that you are smart and can handle some tough questions."

Ida and Dixie decided to ignore my request to stay in the office and came through the swinging door into the bar and dining room area. Dixie huffed. "Ah, see they started without us!"

Cecil eyed Dixie, then looked at me like he was studying an ant on a blade of grass. "Okay. I've got some time to kill. I'll take you up on that drink, too. White Russian."

I yelled to Dixie. "White Russian for Cecil."

Dixie chortled. "Sure he doesn't want try some

peach pie?"

I scowled back at her. "Dixie! Please."

Dixie went about making the drink and I turned back to Cecil. "Ready to start?" Cecil nodded yes to me so I continued. "Mr. Page, can you please tell us how Zach's death has affected you?"

Cecil paused a moment. "Well, it has meant more work. Now that I have to pick up the slack created by his absence." I could see Dixie suppress her desire to punch his throat as she set down his drink.

I continued, "Do you miss him?"

"Of course. He could be a total pain in the you know what. But it is hard without him."

Dixie jumped in. "Zach seemed to specialize in being a pain in the you know what...isn't that what you thought!"

Piper glared at Dixie, but then returned to Cecil and went into full journalist mode. "What do you mean hard without him? Hard as in too much work. Or hard emotionally?" She held our her little voice recorder after asking her question.

Cecil shrugged and looked at the recorder she held in front of him. "A little of both I think."

Guardrail stepped to one side to get a better shot and tripped on the power cable. Digger caught him. Dog yanked on the power cable and bellowed. "Careful. You go over I'm not sure we're getting a guy as big as you and that hulk of a camera back upright."

Guardrail responded. "I'm fine. Keep that line form under my feet."

I cut them off. "Boys, this is not about you. Stop it. Now Cecil, tell me about your relationship with Zach. You worked for him for a while, so you must have known him well."

"Well, that's kind of personal."

I tried to clarify and be more specific. "There are videos of Zach teasing you, being hard on you, all over Youtube. Was that all just in fun and did you have a good relationship?"

Cecil scowled a little and shifted in his seat. "I'm not sure I want to get into that."

I pressed. "Everyone wants to know why he teased you and why those videos are on Youtube."

Cecil rubbed his chin then took a sip of his drink. "I know, but I don't like to talk about that." He paused just a second. "I guess. He could be a little tough on me. But I guess it was okay."

Piper jumped in. "What do you mean tough on you?"

Cecil fidgeted slightly. "Well, he would tease me a lot. And his pranks went over the top sometimes." He paused. "You know I'm not sure I am comfortable with this..."

Piper resumed. "Can you tell me about a prank that went over the top, as you called it?"

Cecil nodded. "I guess. Well one time..."

The front door opened and I was hoping to see Aunt Mae. But a number of the TV crew poured into the pub, led by Scooter. They waved at Cecil sitting at the bar with us and went about their business.

I cleared my throat. "You were saying?"

Cecil continued. "Well one time, we were shooting..."

The front door opened again and this time it was the Sheriff, followed by Aunt Mae and Deputy Wise. The Sheriff rested his hand on his holstered gun. Then Sheriff Morrison used his loud, official voice. "Cecil Page, freeze – don't move. Everyone else, please move away from Mr. Page."

But Cecil didn't freeze. He grabbed Piper around the neck with one arm and barked back at the Sheriff. "No, you stay right there or I will break her neck."

The Sheriff somehow stayed calm and continued. "There is no reason for anyone else to get hurt. Let Piper go and don't make things worse for youself."

The rest of us backed away from Cecil, just a little. Then the impossible happened. The lights did their flickering trick and it went dark. Then I heard a ruckus that ended with a loud thump. The lights came back and I saw Cecil lying on the floor unconscious, covered in pickled eggs. The large jar sat on the floor next to him, unbroken for a change. Piper still stood where she was, trembling. I stepped over to her and took her hands in mine. "Are you alright." Piper nodded yes in return.

"Boss, I can't take this plucking chicken ghost thing anymore. Are you kidding me! And don't even think about blaming a fuse for this one." I had to admit, Dixie had a way with words and the swear jar was going to take some time to refill with her new found language skills.

Guardrail put down the camera and went over to Piper. He put his arm around her and pulled her tight to him. "We would never let that twit hurt you." Piper replied to him with a little sniffle and some tears.

Even though the jar knocked him out cold, the police handcuffed Cecil and called for an ambulance. Then we waited for the medics to come take the trash out of my pub.

Chapter Fourteen

Aunt Mae invited Dad and me to meet her in front of the police station. She mentioned she had a surprise for us. Mae directed us to be there at ten in the morning and wait on the bench out front. We sat watching the beautiful day come to life perched on the old wooden slats. Dad asked, "What do you think she wants?"

"Probably some followup to Cecil's arrest. I'm sure it's nothing big."

"Ginger, you don't know your Aunt Mae as well I as I thought. She is usually not this mysterious with things."

From behind the two of us, we heard Aunt Mae's voice. "You talking about lil ol' me? I can be spontaneous when I want to be, you should know your sister better than that Tom!"

"You haven't been spontaneous since the Rubick's cube was popular."

Mae chuckled. "You calling me old?"

Dad might have blushed a little. "No, of course not. Just saying you like to plan things, no surprises."

Mae smiled. "Not today. I have a surprise for both

of you. I think you earned it. The Sheriff agreed to let us use his horses for the morning. I packed a special picnic and thought we would head down to Bear's Paw swamp. Well that field where the wild flowers grow overlooking the swamp."

"The one mom loved." I had not been there many times since my mother passed.

"The same, sweetie. Let's get mounted up and head out."

Tom snorted. "I'm not sure this old body can ride anymore."

Mae laughed. "That is why you are riding Princess, she is easy to ride."

Dad did not like the sound of that. "And who are you going to ride, then?"

"Trigger, or course." Mae started off for the stalls.

Sheriff Morrison kept three horses he owned, at his own expense, in the stalls with two police horses owned by the town. Potter's Mill encompassed a lot of country, much of which was not accessible by road. The police relied on the horses to get out and patrol many of those areas. The Sheriff loved all the horses and I was shocked Mae got to use them for the morning.

"Ginger, this is Pigpen. He will be your friend for the day." Mae patted the big, brown horse as she spoke.

Dad laughed. "Now I don't feel so bad about riding Princess." Princess was a pretty white spotted breast. She may be a female, but she was bigger than Pigpen.

Mae mounted Trigger and smiled and her whole face lighted up in a way I had not seen in a while. She said, "Now, go ahead, get on. We're burning daylight."

So we put our foot in the stirrups, and rose up into our saddles. It felt good to be on a horse again. After a thirty minute ride, we were at the meadow. It was a beautiful field covered in wild flowers. It was one of my mom's favorite places. It overlooked a stream feeding into the river and provided a clear view of Bear Paw's swamp.

Aunt Mae took a big basket with her and she now placed it on the ground. She took out a large blanket and picked a nice spot to spread it out. Then she moved the basket onto the blanket and opened it up. She took out a container of cornbread, a bowl with pulled pork, and another container with potato salad. She then removed a bag of sandwich rolls and a thermos of iced tea. "This was one of your mom's favs. Pulled pork and cornbread. No sandwich for her, she like to pile the meat on the cornbread and dig in. And the potato salad. She loved the potato salad on the side. She told me once it was her favorite picnic menu."

Dad sighed. "Mae, you shouldn't have. You're a dear lass to remember Jessica and do this. Jess loved this picnic because it was the first one she packed for us as a family. It was all we could afford to do at the time for fun. And we came here when Ginger was a lil sprig. I'm not sure how you knew that, but you clearly did."

Mae pinched her lips. She was touched to see Dad's hard exterior softened, just a little. "Jessica told me that story more than once. And how she would come down here with you, with this same meal packed up, even after Ginger got older and didn't want to be with her parents."

I felt a tear in my eye. I missed my mom and had not taken a moment to remember her in a while. I hugged Aunt Mae and whispered, "Thank you."

Mae patted my back. "I should be thanking you. Without your help we may still be trying to figure out how to arrest Cecil. And you would still have a closed kitchen."

Dad managed to repair the soft spot in his hard shell and his loud, confident voice was back. "She's a chip off the ol' block. A real go getter."

Mae raised her ice tea. "I will second that. Ginger is a doer. And her Dad, well let's just say we love him."

Dad grumbled. "You trying to insult me?"

Mae crinkled her nose. "Maybe more like tease you a little."

I laughed at the two of them. "I want to thank you

Aunt Mae, the last couple of weeks have been, well, tough. This is nice of you to take us out here to relax, be with family. And most important, remember Mom."

Mae nodded. "You're welcome. If you can't rely on family, who can you rely on?"

Dad and I replied in unison. "No one."

Mae laughed and eyed me a moment. "I'm glad you got your kitchen back. And we're both happy those protesters are gone."

Dad scratched his head. "You know, about all this murder business. How did Cecil know Zach was going to pull that prank? How did he know about the powder in the vial? And when to swap it?"

Mae lied on her back and watched the clouds. "That was the one thing Ginger here didn't figure out. Or us for that matter. But Cecil spilled his guts when we got him in an interrogation room. He used the sound meters that Tyler put all over the pub. Or wherever they were shooting. Zach had belittled Cecil so much he was self conscious and figured out how to eavesdrop on the crew using the sound meters. He tapped into them and listened to what others were saying about him."

I sighed. "Dixie was right. He was a little weasel. That is kind of creepy."

Mae put her hands behind her head. "You think that's creepy. Get this, Cecil also kept a list of ways to kill Zach. Then he waited for the right moment. He loved the sodium polyarylate method ever since he saw it on 101 Unique Deaths. So when he heard Zach was going to snort seltzer powder, he jumped on the chance."

I added, "As proven by the DNA testing, and our jar video."

Mae went on. "Well the jar video is interesting. But I'm not sure it would be admissible. And the DA doesn't need it. We have plenty of evidence without the jar video. And speaking of creepy, how on earth did that jar move, sweetie?"

Tom beat me to the response. "It's the chicken. Everyone knows it's our grouchy spirit."

I laughed. "Always the chicken with you."

Dad did not miss a beat. "Then how do you explain the jar moving to one side, then rotating just a little, so that the jar captures the reflection just right? This time you can't blame the cats."

I paused. "I can't. Guess I will need more time to ponder that one."

Mae laughed. "And what about the flying jar! That is even weirder."

Dad huffed. "See, you're ignoring the obvious. The pub is the grumpy chicken's home and he was protecting it."

I laughed, a little. "I don't know, Dad. But it is

odd. I will give you that. Now enjoy some of that pulled pork and corn bread. We need to get back to work soon, so bask in the sun with your wonderful meal and grumpy chicken stories while you can."

Dad looked over to Aunt Mae who had closed her eyes and it looked like we might have bored her to sleep. "You need to go back to work?" Mae nodded no. "Neither do I. But Ginger might. Seems to me like you're the one who needs to soak this all up real quick and get back to work."

I hung my jaw. "That's so mean. You're the owner. Why do I have to go back?"

Dad laughed. "Because I'm the owner still. And you're the manager. I am telling you as the boss."

I eyed him while Aunt Mae laughed. "Dad!"

Dad continued. "And can you put colcannon on the menu? I've had a hankering for that for the last few days. You don't put that on the menu enough."

I snorted. "I don't know. I'm just the help it seems. I'll have to get permission to order the cabbage."

Mae intervened. "Don't be like Cecil. He's just joshing ya. It's his way of letting you know you run that place without admitting it."

Dad laughed. "I wouldn't let my little girl ride back alone. You know that. Mae's right, I'm just teasing ya."

I leaned over to Dad and hugged him. "It's nice to

know I am loved."

Dad barked. "I didn't say that!"

Mae sat up a little to stare at Dad. "Now, be nice you ol' dog. This is a nice moment. And, sweetie, that is as close as you'll get to an 'I love you' from him. We both know it."

Dad nodded. "Glad that is cleared up."

All three of us laughed and went back to our food and drink. Aunt Mae made the best iced tea and I made a mental note to talk to her about it. A nice ice tea on our menu would not be a bad addition for a pub in a small southern town.

Later as we saddled up and prepared to leave, I looked back at the wild flowers. Under my breath I said, "I miss you, Mom. And I promise I'll come back here more often."

Chapter Fifteen

The state labs completed work on the powder samples Mae took from Cecil's fingers. And to no one's surprise, the white substance was slush powder, or as the police called it sodium polyacrylate. That combined with the DNA results from the paper bag were pretty solid. But the police combined that evidence with the order Cecil placed for the magician's kit and the pickled egg jar video to charge him. The district attorney in Atlanta said it was a strong case.

The Ghost Hounds wrapped up their shoot and packed it up to move on to the next location – less a few crew members. Cecil was in custody; Zach was dead; and Ida was out of town with Scooter. The new minted couple decided a "vacation" was in order and headed out for a secluded cabin on the island of Tortola to relax. My computer oriented pain in the neck was not the only one to leave town with the TV show. The protesters were gone too. And to my satisfaction the town seemed to be close to normal again.

I was behind the bar and glanced at the new monitor set up by Scooter as a parting present to us. If was a large, flat screen that looked nicer than I expected over the bar. On it, we currently looped the video shot by Guardrail during Cecil's arrest.

Dixe made some drinks and watched a little of the video. "Guardrail is lucky he's good at custom motorcycles. He stinks as a cameraman. He cuts off your head in the first shot, trips at one point so we get a good look at the ceiling, and talks while shooting."

I looked up to watch again. I think I had seen it a hundred times by now. "You got to give him credit. He kept shooting right through the darkness, even though the power went out for a few seconds, and he got all the footage of the actual arrest. The shot of Cecil on the floor with all those pickled eggs and juice all over him, out cold, was pretty good."

"More like hilarious." Dixie laughed.

"I'm not sure any of this is funny to me, Dixie. It's so sad that so many lives were turned upside down."

Dixie turned to me, losing her bartender demeanor. She put her arm around me. "I know. And that is why you need to enjoy Star's concert tonight. I hear she wrote a song about all of this and it supposed to be pretty good."

"I hope so. The crowd is starting to gather, and it looks like we're going to be packed."

Dixie let me go and clapped. "Great. I can use the tips."

"I'm glad to see you're back to normal."

Time passed quickly as Dixie and Tom made drinks together. Then Star showed up early for her big performance and she was a ball of energy. And the crowd grew. It seems with the protesters gone, everyone wanted to be in The Grumpy Chicken for her show.

I rested at a table with Piper, next to Lily and Edith's table. This seemed to be the seating order now; Lily and Edith held court at their table with Piper and me at the next table, plus Ida when she wasn't on vacation. The boys had reclaimed their seats at the bar, but came over to sit with Lily and Edith to be part of the current discussion.

Piper was talking to Lily and Edith. "I thought he was going to kill me. But when it went dark. Something hit him, I think it was the jar, and he just fell to the ground."

Guardrail added. "You were lucky you didn't get hit by it."

Dog jumped in. "Not luck. It was the chicken ghost helping out."

Piper nodded. "I hate to say it, Dog. Even though the fancy camera Scooter lent us went out with the lights, the jar webcam caught the container flying off the counter even though it was dark. Ida said it ran on the laptop's battery and it has low light sensing. You can see the jar just clearly flies off the counter, out of frame. We have to assume it hit Cecil just right in the head to knock him out. So, yeah, it's beyond explanation. A chicken ghost is as good a guess as any."

I had to bite my tongue. There was no blaming a cat for this incident.

Digger shook his head. "Who would have thought a clumsy, chubby guy like Cecil could be so devious."

Edith waved her hand, like she was turning a page. "Who knows what darkness lurks in the hearts of men. What a shame this all had to happen. But it's all over now."

Dog raised his voice. "Hey, I was right again. It was a ghost hit man."

Guardrail scrunched up his face. "Not even close this time, Dog. The killer was Cecil. The flying jar may be because of the chicken ghost but it didn't kill anyone."

Dog pulled back. "Yeah, I guess. But a ghost was involved."

Piper said, "I was trying to write up the story last night, but I'm not sure how to explain the flying jar. I'm not sure I believe it was the chicken ghost, but I haven't ruled it out either."

Digger responded. "That's a good summary, Piper. And that's always the way with the chicken ghost. Kind of, maybe, but never certain."

Piper laughed. "I have to think about it some more, Digger, but you're right about it being uncertain and I cannot write it up if I'm not sure. The one thing I do know, I am so glad it is over and no one else got hurt. Especially me!"

Star came over and sat with Piper and me. "I am so excited. I had another vision into the fog the other night when the arrest happened. I could feel a spirit presence that was angry at someone acting badly. I wrote a song about it and want to play it for you tonight."

I laughed. "An Irish ballad about a Potter's Mill chicken spirit. That's not something you hear every day."

Star gushed. "No it isn't. But The Grumpy Chicken is not your normal pub. I knew that when I opened up next door. And I'm glad I did. It's the perfect place for a new age store. That reminds me Ginger, we should talk about marketing and merchandising at some point. There lots of people interested in this place now. And the paranormal. We might be able to generate some business together."

I hesitated. "I don't know Star. That sounds like it's out of my league. I'm a simple pub owner."

Dad's voice boomed. He had a way of walking up at the right time. "Correction. You're the manager, I'm still the owner as long as I'm breathing."

I sniped at him. "I see the sensitive, considerate dad is never going to happen, is it?"

Piper patted my hand on the table. "That's about as good as it gets with him."

I smiled at her. "I know, but I can still hope!"

Dad went on. "Star, I have some ideas. But I need to know more about those visions of yours. You poor lil lass."

I interrupted. "Dad, Star has to play a concert. We

have plenty of time to talk business later."

Dog broke his silence. "Yeah, I think we need some more drinks."

Guardrail tilted his head. "You buying?"

"Heck, no! This is Digger's round. I lost my shirt on bets with this one. No one wants to cut me some slack even though a ghost *was* involved. It's just a technicality the ghost wasn't a hit man"

Digger chuckled. "Dog, you never want to pay on a debt. That is one of your weaker excuses. The murderer was Cecil. You lost. Now pay up."

"I'll pay up as long as you buy the next round." Dog held up his empty mug.

Digger mumbled. "Alright. But pay up first." Dog threw a twenty on the table and Digger rose to head to the bar.

I let them go this time. If I told them betting was not allowed in the bar, they still would gamble. It was a waste of breath. And besides, the boys were acting normal again and I was taking all the normal I could get.

The only abnormal thing I allowed tonight was the removal of about a third of the dining room tables. As requested by Star, we made a large empty space in front of our makeshift stage to serve as a dance floor. I was curious to see if anyone would use it.

To my amazement, once Star starting playing her

guitar the first two dancers hit the floor – Edith and Lily. We all just stared at the odd sight of the two spinster sisters dancing with each other. And no one was bold enough to tell them they did not know how to dance. After a minute or so, I saw a few couples join them on the floor and before long, the dance floor was full. In fact, it was too small for all the people. Seems Star knew her audience when she asked for the dance floor.

Star's music was loud, but it was not rock concert deafening and I could hear Dixie's loud, sturdy voice over the music. She was waving the bar's land line phone. I was not happy to see that and assumed the worst. I went over to the bar and answered.

"Hello. Ginger? This is Jacob. I know it's been a long time, but I am selling a new line of liquors and your town is in my territory. I was hoping to make a sales call if you would be willing to give me an appointment."

I paused. "Jacob, the divorce went about as smooth as something like that can go. But I'm not sure I want to do business with my ex-husband."

"Oh come on! What have you got to lose. I can sell you some of the good stuff at a price no one else can match. It will be worth your time. And why is it so loud there?"

"We're having a concert. Star from next door is playing. It's not a good time. Can we talk tomorrow, when it's not so hectic."

"Sure. I'll call you back tomorrow." Then Jacob hung up.

I looked over to Dixie. "You're not going to believe this. Jacob wants to make a sales call to us."

Dixie laughed and looked over Dad's way. "You better not even let Tom know, he doesn't like your ex at all."

"Why can't things be normal for just one night?"

Dixie threw her hands in the air. "This is a normal night. You can't let one little phone call upset you. Here, look at this." She opened the register drawer. It was full.

"Wow. We're having a good night."

Dixie pinched my cheek. "See. Relax and have some fun."

"One, don't pinch my cheek ever again. That hurts more than I remembered. And two, if I get grumpy like the chicken again, show me that drawer once more. I've been so worried about our bills with the slow days we had. This will help."

"There ya go. Want me to make ya a drink?"

"Nah. I think I might just go help Bones on the grill. He's been working pretty hard back there and he could use some help. Besides, it feels normal to me when I work the grill."

Dixie laughed. "No one can accuse you of living

the glamorous life."

I smiled back. "No, they can't. But it's the life I want and love." I headed off to help Bones and be normal. For at least a little while.

Thanks for reading! I hope you enjoyed the book and it would mean so much to me if you could leave a review. Reviews help authors gain more exposure and keep us writing your favorite stories.

You can find all of my books by visiting my Author Page.

Sign up for Constance Barker's New Releases Newsletter where you can find out when my next book is coming out and for special discounted pricing.

I never share or sell your email.

Visit me on Facebook and give me feedback on the characters and their stories.

The Grumpy Chicken Irish Pub Series

A Frosty Mug of Murder

Old School Diner Cozy Mysteries

Murder at Stake

Murder Well Done

A Side Order of Deception

Murder, Basted and Barbecued

The Curiosity Shop Cozy Mysteries

The Curious Case of the Cursed Spectacles

The Curious Case of the Cursed Dice

The Curious Case of the Cursed Dagger

The Curious Case of the Cursed Looking Glass

The We're Not Dead Yet Club

Fetch a Pail of Murder

Wedding Bells and Death Knells

Murder or Bust

Pinched, Pilfered and a Pitchfork

A Hot Spot of Murder

Witchy Women of Coven Grove Series

The Witching on the Wall

A Witching Well of Magic

Witching the Night Away

Witching There's Another Way

Witching Your Life Away

Witching You Wouldn't Go

Witching for a Miracle

Teasen & Pleasen Hair Salon Series

A Hair Raising Blowout

Wash, Rinse, Die

Holiday Hooligans

Color Me Dead

False Nails & Tall Tales

Caesar's Creek Series

A Frozen Scoop of Murder (Caesars Creek Mystery Series Book One)

Death by Chocolate Sundae (Caesars Creek Mystery Series Book Two)

Soft Serve Secrets (Caesars Creek Mystery Series Book Three)

Ice Cream You Scream (Caesars Creek Mystery Series Book Four)

Double Dip Dilemma (Caesars Creek Mystery Series Book Five)

Melted Memories (Caesars Creek Mystery Series Book Six)

Triple Dip Debacle(Caesars Creek Mystery Series Book Seven)

Whipped Wedding Woes(Caesars Creek Mystery Series Book Eight)

A Sprinkle of Tropical Trouble(Caesars Creek Mystery Series Book Nine)

A Drizzle of Deception(Caesars Creek Mystery Series Book Ten)

Sweet Home Mystery Series

Creamed at the Coffee Cabana (Sweet Home Mystery Series Book One)

A Caffeinated Crunch (Sweet Home Mystery Series Book Two)

A Frothy Fiasco (Sweet Home Mystery Series Book Three)

Punked by the Pumpkin(Sweet Home Mystery Series Book Four)

Peppermint Pandemonium(Sweet Home Mystery Series Book Five)

Expresso Messo(Sweet Home Mystery Series Book Six)

A Cuppa Cruise Conundrum(Sweet Home Mystery Series Book Seven)

The Brewing Bride(Sweet Home Mystery Series Book Eight)

Whispering Pines Mystery Series

A Sinister Slice of Murder

Sanctum of Shadows (Whispering Pines Mystery Series)

Curse of the Bloodstone Arrow (Whispering Pines Mystery Series)

Fright Night at the Haunted Inn (Whispering Pines Mystery Series)

Mad River Mystery Series

A Wicked Whack

A Prickly Predicament

A Malevolent Menace

40153051R00093

Made in the USA
Columbia, SC
12 December 2018